'You're not really my type, Doyle!'

'Is that so?' he mocked.

Gabrielle slid her gaze over him almost insultingly. 'I like my men to have a bit more . . . finesse.'

With a speed which shocked her Doyle had Gabrielle in his arms. 'So I leave you cold, do I, Gabby? My lack of finesse is a turn-off?'

'Yes!' she spat.

Doyle drew back. 'I can make you want me, Gabby. We both know that.'

Dear Reader

Spring is here at last—a time for new beginnings and time, perhaps, finally to start putting all those New Year's resolutions into action! Whatever your plans, don't forget to look out this month for a wonderful selection of romances from the exotic Amazon, Australia, the Americas and enchanting Italy. Our resolution remains, as always, to bring you the best in romance from around the world!

The Editor

Jennifer Taylor was born in Liverpool, England, and still lives in the north-west, several miles outside the city. Books have always been a passion of hers, so it seemed natural to choose a career in librarianship, a wise decision as the library is where she met her husband, Bill. Twenty years and two children later, they are still happily married, with the added bonus that she has discovered how challenging and enjoyable writing romantic fiction can be!

Recent titles by the same author:

JUNGLE FEVER

BY
JENNIFER TAYLOR

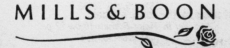

MILLS & BOON

MILLS & BOON LIMITED
ETON HOUSE, 18-24 PARADISE ROAD
RICHMOND, SURREY TW9 1SR

*MILLS & BOON and the Rose Device
are trademarks of the publisher.*

*First published in Great Britain 1995
by Mills & Boon Limited*

© Jennifer Talyor 1995

*Australian copyright 1995   Philippine copyright 1995
This edition 1995*

ISBN 0 263 78933 0

*Set in Times Roman 10 on 12 pt.
01-9504-56318 C*

Made and printed in Great Britain

CHAPTER ONE

THE sun was blisteringly hot.

Gabrielle lifted the heavy weight of rich chestnut-coloured hair from her neck and wiped away the trickles of perspiration with a lace-edged handkerchief. Wadding the soiled cotton square into a ball, she pushed it back into the pocket of her fashionably short white linen skirt then glanced across the clearing.

The man was still sitting on the oil-drum, calmly whittling away at a stick, as he'd been doing for the best part of an hour now. He looked totally relaxed, despite the heat which had left damp patches on his khaki shirt, and, unreasonably, Gabrielle felt her temper start to rise.

She stood up, easing the red silk blouse away from her hot skin as she crossed the few yards which separated them and stopped in front of him. He must have heard her approaching across the dry, dusty grass but he didn't look up, just carried on whittling slivers off the wood with that wicked-looking bone-handled knife. And Gabrielle's temper moved another notch up the scale.

'How much longer is it going to take?'

He looked up then, those strange silvery-blue eyes, which made such a startling contrast to his tanned skin and dark brown hair, resting on her stormy face for a brief moment before he turned his attention back to the knife in his hands. 'As long as it needs to. Why don't

5

you go and sit back down in the shade, Miss Marshall? You look kind of hot.'

She was more than just hot, she was blazing now, and it owed little to the heat of the midday sun. Reaching out, she snatched the stick from his hands and tossed it on to the ground, her grey eyes glittering with anger. 'My grandfather hired you to fly me out to where he is staying. Now, I suggest you start doing something towards earning your money!'

He stood up, uncoiling his length from the oil-drum until he seemed to tower over her, and despite her anger Gabrielle felt a certain trepidation. There was something intimidating about the man. She had felt it from the moment he had met her at the airport in Mexico City, although he had said very little. He had merely handed her the letter of introduction from her grandfather, then escorted her to that disreputable Jeep, which was now languishing in the shade at the other side of the clearing. It had been on the tip of her tongue to refuse to travel in the broken-down vehicle, but one look at the man's face had stopped her protests dead. Yet what was it about him that made her feel so wary?

In a lightning-fast journey her eyes took stock, from feet encased in well-worn boots, up long, muscular legs, over narrow hips and a trim waist to the chest covered in the sweat-stained shirt. The damp material clung, outlining every flat muscle, and she felt a strange little tightening in the pit of her stomach before deliberately lifting her gaze to the harsh, angular lines of the man's face and those disturbingly light eyes. He wasn't a handsome man by any means, his features being too tough and unrelenting for that, but he exuded a raw masculinity which Gabrielle found deeply unsettling. The

men in her social set were better-looking, more sophisticated, groomed to perfection—yet not one of them
made her feel so overwhelmingly conscious of being a
woman. It wasn't a feeling she was sure she enjoyed.

'Your grandfather hired me to fly some cargo out to
him. You, Miss Marshall, are merely an addition to the
cargo.'

She couldn't believe her ears. Didn't he realise who
she was? 'And you are making one very big mistake if
you think you can speak to me like that!' She tossed her
head to shake the heavy chestnut waves back from her
face as she glared at him. 'Do you have any idea what
would happen if I told my grandfather how rude you
were to me? You could forget about this two-bit operation of yours, for a start. No one would hire you to
shift "cargo" once Henry Marshall put the word about.'

'Rude? I don't recall being rude to you, lady. Not as
rude as I could be if I really set my mind to it.' He bent
and stared into her face, his eyes like ice as they met
hers from the space of mere inches. 'Frankly I think it's
way past time someone put you in your place and made
you realise that you can't walk all over people just because your family has more money than it knows what
to do with.'

'Why, you insolent...!' Her hand came up, her intention obvious, but the man made no attempt to avoid
the stinging slap. He smiled slowly, his eyes boring into
hers in a way which made her feel suddenly ashamed.
Even as she watched she could see the mark left by her
hand changing from white to red on his lean, tanned
cheek. She looked away but he caught her chin, forcing
her to look straight at him and acknowledge what she
had done.

'That was the one and only time that you will do that and get away with it. Understand?' His fingers were surprisingly gentle yet Gabrielle knew that she would never be able to free herself without a struggle. She drew in a shaky breath, wanting desperately to refuse to answer him, but one look at the cold determination in those pale eyes told her that that would be another mistake.

'Yes!'

'Good. We seem to be starting to make some progress now. Let's call it the first step towards a greater understanding of each other, shall we, Miss Marshall?'

There seemed to be an undertone to the statement, yet she had no idea what it was. When he released her she hurried back across the clearing and sat down again on the log. She was trembling all over, her whole body convulsing with tiny spasms as though each nerve had been rubbed rawly sensitive. Why on earth had Grandfather hired such a man? He could have had his pick, yet he had chosen him. It was just one more strange thing to add to all the others Henry Marshall had done lately, starting with his announcing that he was retiring and moving to Brazil to mine for amethysts!

She tipped her head back against the trunk of the tree and closed her eyes, going over it all in her head, but it was still impossible to understand why he had made such a crazy decision. That man was right—her family did have more money than they could spend in a hundred lifetimes, earned from the huge chemical business her grandfather had founded fifty years before. Yet that didn't explain why, at the age of seventy-two, he had suddenly decided to turn his back on it all and go to South America.

Gabrielle had been staying with friends in New York when her mother had telephoned, nearly hysterical as she'd informed her of the old man's decision. It had been partly to calm her mother down that Gabrielle had offered to fly out and try to reason with him. She and her grandfather had always been close; her own father had died when she was just a child and her grandfather had taken an interest in everything she did, although recently she had seen little of him. As one of the élite few who had no need to work she spent her life pursuing pleasure: skiing in Aspen, sailing off the South of France, shopping in New York and Paris and London.

Yet, increasingly in the past few months, Gabrielle had started to wonder if it wasn't a rather pointless existence, if there should be more to her life than a ceaseless search for entertainment. But what? She'd thought hard about it but had so far failed to discover what it was that was missing, the worthwhile direction she could turn her talents towards. This journey to make her grandfather see sense was a way to quieten her increasingly noisy conscience. It was just a pity she would have to make it in such disagreeable company!

She opened her eyes and glanced across at the man, then flushed when she saw that he was watching her. Hurriedly she looked away, pleating the smooth linen skirt between her fingers, and jumped when a deep voice suddenly spoke beside her.

'We shall be leaving in a few minutes. You'd better get your bags out of the Jeep.'

He moved quietly for such a big man. She hadn't heard him approaching and now she could feel her heart hammering in a way which shocked her by its very unexpectedness. Why should he make her feel so on edge,

so...*aware* of him? It didn't make sense. She sailed
through life, untouched by most of it, money and con-
nections smoothing her path and ensuring her the most
deferential treatment wherever she went, yet none of that
seemed to mean anything to him. And it was that more
than anything which pushed her into replying in a way
she knew would provoke him.

'I don't carry bags. That's your job.' She stood up,
smoothing the skirt over her shapely hips as she walked
past him without a second glance. Yet, when she reached
the small plane being wheeled out on to the tarmac
runway, she couldn't resist looking back and experienced a quite irrational sense of disappointment when
she saw him walking towards the Jeep. Had her previous
threats got through to him and made him realise the pre-
cariousness of his position? They must have if he was
meekly fetching her cases. But she felt somehow let
down, as though he had failed some test and slipped in
her estimation of him, and that was ridiculous when she
knew nothing at all about him.

It was another fifteen minutes before they finally took
off. Gabrielle sat in the cockpit and fanned herself with
a magazine while she watched the man run through the
pre-flight check-list with an assurance which would have
allayed any fears she might have had. He was obviously
an experienced pilot, taking time to check that everything was functioning correctly now. There had been
some trouble with a fuel line, he had informed her when
they'd first arrived at the small private airfield on the
outskirts of the city, but obviously that had been sorted
out.

Take-off was smooth and Gabrielle settled back in the
seat, opening the magazine and making a great show out

of reading it to avoid the necessity of making polite conversation. Frankly there was little she could think of to talk about with any degree of civility after their previous run-in. Yet, despite being determined to ignore him, she found her eyes drawn back to him time and again, watching the easy competence he displayed in flying the plane. It was only when he suddenly looked round and caught her staring, and raised a mocking black brow, that she finally made herself look away.

They landed to refuel and Gabrielle didn't bother to wait as she climbed out of the cockpit. She headed straight for the rest-room and took her time washing her sticky hands and face then re-applying a light make-up. When she returned to the small lounge area the man was leaning against the coffee-machine, talking to another pilot. He glanced round as she appeared, his gaze little short of insulting as it skimmed the slender length of her bare legs, the shapely curves shown to perfection by the expensive clothing, then calmly dismissed her.

Gabrielle felt her blood boil at the deliberate lack of interest. She wasn't vain but she knew that she was beautiful. She only had to look in the mirror and see the perfect oval face with its delicate features, the huge, deep grey eyes in their frame of thick sooty lashes and the generously sweet curve of her mouth to know that. Yet that man had looked at her with all the interest he might have afforded a . . . a side of beef!

Curbing her anger, she crossed the room, ignoring him completely as she fed coins into the machine for a cup of coffee. She took a sip and grimaced at its bitter, powdery taste.

'We're leaving in two minutes, so hurry up.'

She barely spared him a glance as she took another leisurely sip out of the plastic cup, then set it down to study the range of confectionery on offer from the machine.

'Did you hear me?' His fingers were hard on her bare arm and surprisingly cool, and she shivered slightly as she moved away to break the contact.

'I'm not deaf. Of course I heard you. However, I'm afraid you will just have to wait a bit longer.' She smiled up into his hard face with a saccharine sweetness. 'I haven't finished my coffee yet, as I'm sure you can see.'

'No?' He returned her smile, but there was little amusement in the slow curl of his chiselled lips. Reaching over, he lifted the cup from where it was standing on top of the machine and calmly emptied the contents into the bin, then crumpled the plastic container in his hand and tossed it in as well. 'I rather think you have finished it now, Miss Marshall, don't you? Now, come along.'

He turned to leave but Gabrielle had no intention of letting him get away with that! She caught hold of his arm, uncaring that her French-manicured nails dug into his flesh through the thin cotton shirt. 'How dare you? Just who do you think you are?'

He tuned round to face her, his silver-blue eyes glittering as they skimmed her angry face before he calmly unfastened her fingers from his arm. 'I am the guy who is flying you out to see your grandfather. Now, I'm not quite sure about the ethics of it, or if that gives me the same sort of authority that the captain of a ship has, but humour me, Miss Marshall, please. When I say that we are leaving, then leave we shall.'

He slid a hand under her chin and lifted her face so that he could look straight into her eyes, and Gabrielle felt a wave of heat flow through her at the expression on his face and the tone in his deep voice. 'I'm sure you wouldn't like the way that I deal with mutiny.'

He let her go, the doors swinging to behind him as he headed back to the plane. Gabrielle ran a hand over her face, shaken to the core by what had happened. He hadn't hurt her, his touch having been too gentle to inflict bruises, yet she could feel her flesh throbbing where his fingers had been, echoing the throbbing deep inside her as she remembered the strange sensuality of that threat he had issued. Having him speak to her that way should have made her spitting mad with fury, but that wasn't how she felt. If she was honest then she had to admit that she felt afraid—not just of him, but of her own strange reactions. The sooner this trip was over the better!

She didn't expect to be able to relax after what had passed between them but the total lack of conversation combined with the droning of the engines for mile after mile took effect. She fell into a light doze, to be awoken abruptly some time later when the plane dipped alarmingly.

She sat bolt upright, staring down at the undulating vista of forest below, then gasped when the plane took another dive towards the ground. 'What is it? What's happening?'

'Fuel line again. Looks as though it's starting to play up.' The man's face was set, his hands moving over the controls as he lifted the radio handset and started barking out a string of numbers Gabrielle couldn't follow.

'You don't think we're going to crash, do you?' Her voice was shrill with fear and she felt him glance at her before he looked down at the ground as he turned the plane in a slow, steady circle.

'Not crash, Miss Marshall.'

'Thank God!' She eased her grip on the seat, then gave a little scream as she saw the treetops coming up to meet them. 'I thought you said we weren't going to crash.'

'And so we aren't. But we're coming down. We have no choice.'

'Down? In all those trees? It's impossible.'

He reached across the space and turned her head to the right, his fingers hard and strangely reassuring against her cheek. 'There's a clearing down there. I'm going to land in that.'

He put both hands back on the controls and Gabrielle closed her eyes and prayed, then gave a sharp cry of fear when she felt the wheels touch the ground before the plane bumped back up into the air. Twice more the plane skimmed the rough surface, then slowly came to an unsteady halt on the very edge of the small clearing. Gabrielle counted to ten then opened her eyes and looked around.

Green. That was all she could see—trees, shrubs, foliage—acres upon acres of dense greenery, which looked impenetrable to her eyes.

'Where...where are we?' Her voice was low but the man obviously heard her as he switched off the engines and unclipped his seatbelt. He pushed open the cockpit door then glanced back at her and shrugged.

'Somewhere in the middle of Brazil by my reckonings.'

'Somewhere?' Her voice had risen. She caught his shoulder when he would have climbed out and stopped him. 'Don't you know exactly where?'

'Not exactly, no. The compass went on the blink a while back.'

'But didn't you give out a map reference just before we came down, over the radio?'

'Yes, but it wasn't accurate. It was the last one I had taken so I broadcast it on the assumption that it was better than nothing.'

She couldn't believe what she was hearing. They had landed in the middle of the jungle and the likelihood was that no one had the faintest idea where they were!

When he climbed out of the plane she followed him, staring round at the wall of greenery. 'But what are we going to do? How long will it take for people to find us?'

He reached behind his seat and dragged out a battered leather bag, and dropped it unceremoniously on to the ground. 'It's hard to say. A couple of days, a week…two. Could be more.'

'Two weeks? But we can't stay here that long!'

He smiled suddenly, his face creasing into an attractive smile which made an instant and quite unwanted shiver of appreciation ripple down her spine. 'We certainly can't. I'm pleased to see that you're taking such a sensible view of it all.'

She didn't feel sensible, anything but! But there was no way she was going to let him know that. 'Then what are we going to do?'

'Surely it's obvious.' He unzipped the bag and started to rummage through the contents, dragging out a pair of khaki trousers and a shirt identical to the ones he was wearing. 'They'll be big on you, but you only have yourself to blame.'

He was talking in riddles—either that or the shock had affected her ability to follow even simple statements. Gabrielle stared at the clothing he held out to her, then looked up at him and shrugged. 'I'm sorry but I have no idea what you're talking about.'

He rolled the clothes into a ball and tossed them at her feet, then started collecting items from the plane and placing them in a tidy heap on the ground. 'You didn't bring your bags with you so you will have to wear some of my things.' He skimmed a look up her bare legs and down to her feet in the strappy leather sandals. 'Shoes are going to be a problem, though, unless...'

He dragged a pair of deplorable battered plimsolls from under the seat of the plane and tossed them to her. Gabrielle let them fall to the ground, staring at them with huge, disbelieving eyes. 'Do you mean to say that you...you *left* my cases in the Jeep?'

'*I* didn't leave them. You had your chance to put them on board and you chose not to. The blame is yours.' There was an edge of steel in his deep voice but Gabrielle was so incensed that she ignored it.

'It was up to you to do that! You were hired to fly me down here.'

'But I wasn't hired to act as your valet.' There was contempt in his pale eyes as they met her stormy ones. 'You're a big girl now. I'm sure you're capable of performing a simple little task like dealing with your own luggage. Now, I suggest that you stop complaining and get yourself into those things.'

Gabrielle took a deep breath and held it. She felt like screaming only she had the feeling that he wouldn't take a scrap of notice if she did. She'd never felt so helpless in her life! 'Forgive me for sounding stupid, but why should I want to wear your clothes?' She poked the bundle of clothing with her toe, her face mirroring distaste. 'I hardly think they're going to suit me, do you?'

He crouched down and rapidly packed the items he'd collected into a rucksack, swinging it on to his back as he straightened. 'They're definitely not from Dior, Miss Marshall, but I'm sure you'll find them far more suitable than the outfit you're wearing—fetching though it may be.' He glanced past her at the wall of greenery. 'You can get some very nasty cuts and grazes in there.'

Gabrielle followed his gaze and felt her heart start to pound in a rhythm which made her feel sick. 'You don't mean that you expect me to go into that...that jungle?'

He shrugged as he settled the heavy bag more comfortably across his shoulders. 'I don't expect anything. It's up to you what you do. However, there is no way that I'm waiting around here for a rescue which might never happen.' He sliced her a cool glance. 'The choice is yours...again. You can either come with me or stay here. Make up your mind.'

'But I...' She swallowed down the words, then tried again, desperate to make him see sense. 'Look, Mr——' She stopped abruptly, her face flaming as she suddenly realised that she didn't even know his name, and saw him smile with a biting contempt.

'So you finally got around to wondering about it, did you? The name's Doyle, for your information, Miss Marshall.'

The icy tone in his deep voice stung, and she glared back. 'If I had realised you were such a stickler for etiquette then I would have asked sooner, *Mr Doyle*. You really must forgive me for the oversight.'

If he heard her sarcasm he ignored it as he drew the knife from its sheath and started towards the wall of trees. He paused on the edge of the clearing, looking back at her with a faint, almost indifferent lift of one brow. 'It's make your mind up time, lady. Are you coming or not?'

Gabrielle stared back at him, then looked around the small open patch of land. The jungle seemed to press in on her from all sides, dark and oppressive, the steamy heat from the vegetation filling the air with a dank odour. She didn't want to enter that green world, yet neither did she want to stay here by herself.

It was only when she heard the hissing slash of the knife cutting a path through the greenery that she roused herself, just in time to see Doyle's broad back disappearing. With a small cry of alarm Gabrielle scooped up the bundle of clothes and ran after him.

There was a saying about better the devil you know, but somehow she couldn't draw a whole lot of comfort from it. She knew nothing at all about this particular devil, in the form of a man called Doyle!

CHAPTER TWO

'I'M TIRED. I don't think I can go any further. Did you hear me?'

Gabrielle's voice rose an octave, annoyance rippling through it, as she watched Doyle hack another branch off the plant. He glanced round at her, wiping the sweat from his forehead with the back of his arm, those pale eyes studying her in a way which made her feel like some particularly nasty kind of specimen.

Gabrielle drew herself up to her full height, trying not to imagine how ridiculous she must look. They'd been walking for hours now, their progress hampered by the thickness of the trees. Every foot forward had been a struggle, the plants clawing at their clothing, seemingly intent on holding them back. There were streaks of dirt all over her white skirt, a rip in the back of her silk blouse and her feet were filthy with encrusted mud. She wanted nothing more than to lie down on the floor and scream at the hand fate had dealt her, only something about the way that damned man was watching her prevented her from doing that.

'Ten minutes. That's all you can have, and if I were you, Miss Marshall, I'd use them to change out of those clothes.'

He dug the point of the knife into a nearby stem, then crouched down on his heels, ignoring Gabrielle completely. Despite the strenuous exercise involved in cutting a path through the jungle, he looked little different than

he had when they'd set out. Even as she watched he
closed his eyes, his big body totally at ease. They could
have been out for an afternoon stroll in Kew Gardens
for all the concern he was displaying and, although she
knew it was unfair, Gabrielle felt her temper rise.

'Is that all you can say? Surely you can understand
the seriousness of our situation, Mr Doyle?'

'Just make that Doyle. Forget the Mr. And I am in
no doubt as to how serious this is. However, getting hysterical about it won't help, believe me.'

'Then what will help?' Gabrielle tossed the crumpled
bundle of clothing on to the ground and stared round,
not that there was much to see through the green gloom.
'This whole idea is ridiculous! We should never have left
the plane. I'm going to go back.'

Doyle tipped his head back, watching her through
slitted eyes. 'What for? What do you think you'll find
there—that is *if* you find the plane again?'

'What do you mean, if? All I need to do is retrace
our route. We could be back there in no time and then...'

'Then we sit there and wait for the cavalry to come
along and rescue us? Sorry, Gabby, that isn't going to
happen.'

'The name is Gabrielle! No one calls me Gabby.'

'More's the pity. If someone had done then maybe
you would have turned out a damned sight better than
you have.'

'Now you look here, you...'

He rose to his feet, staring back at her in a way that
made the words dam in her throat. 'No, *you* look here,
lady. This isn't a jaunt down Park Avenue or Bond
Street. You can't just call yourself a cab to get home. If
we are going to have any hope of being found then we

need to get back to where I plotted that last map reference. That's where any search will be centred. I'm going to make my way back there and you're free to come with me. The choice is yours.'

'You would really abandon me here?' She gave a cold little laugh, not bothering to hide her contempt. 'No, don't waste your breath answering that. We both know that you would!'

'Then there doesn't seem to be any point in discussing it further, does there?' He turned his back on her as he picked up the knife again and started to hack away at the trees. Gabrielle watched him in silence, then glanced around. The temptation to tell him to go to hell was immense and she would have done it without a qualm if only she were a hundred per cent certain that she could find her way back to the plane—but she wasn't. The jungle seemed to have already closed over the path Doyle had cut through it, making it difficult to decide which was the right way to go.

She sighed heavily, unrolling the creased bundle of clothes and studying them with distaste before calling to the man who was hacking away at the foliage. 'You'll have to wait while I get changed.'

He turned back, his pale eyes resting on her faintly mutinous face for a moment before he nodded curtly. 'Fair enough. Be as quick as you can.'

Gabrielle smiled cuttingly at him, her hands moving to the tiny buttons on the front of her grubby silk shirt. 'Why? Do you have an urgent appointment someplace? I would have thought we had all the time in the world, and certainly enough to spare me a few minutes to get changed in.'

'I'm afraid that's where you are wrong, lady. We don't have all the time in the world at all.' He ran his thumb down the blade of the knife to wipe away the sap from its shiny surface, then spared her another cool glance. 'Any rescue planes that are sent out won't hang around forever. We need to get back to that spot just as soon as we can or we can forget about being picked up.'

'I... But that's ridiculous! They won't just abandon us here! My... my grandfather will see that that doesn't happen!' It was hard to disguise her horror and she saw him smile in a way which sent a little shiver of alarm racing down her spine.

'I'm sure he'll do everything within his power to get you back, Gabby, but even he will see the sense in curtailing the search after a reasonable length of time has elapsed.' He paused, then continued smoothly, 'Quite a few planes have gone down in this area over the years and not all of them have been found.'

Gabrielle looked away, swallowing down the surge of fear. They *would* be found! The thought of anything else was too much to bear. Her fingers shook as she unbuttoned the blouse and started to peel it down her arms to toss it on to the ground.

'You had better save that. It's a very noticeable colour and could be useful if we need to signal to any planes flying overhead. Here, give it to me and I'll put it in the bag.'

He reached out to take the blouse from her but Gabrielle backed away at once, holding the flimsy garment in front of her, only just becoming aware of the fact that she was standing there half naked in front of him. 'Do you mind? I'm not here to provide you with a free show. Please turn around until I've finished!'

His mouth curled into a slow smile, his pale eyes glittering with barely concealed amusement as they skimmed her. 'What are you worried about? That the sight of you will drive me wild with lust?' He shook his head. 'Sorry, lady, you aren't my type at all, but if you feel safer...'

He turned his back on her, leaning indolently against a tree-trunk, his attitude one of boredom. Gabrielle glared at the broad expanse of his back, wondering why she should feel so annoyed—not at what he had done by watching her but at what he had said! He had dismissed her beauty with a curtness which was insulting. What would he say if she told him that there were dozens of men who would have sold their soul to get a glimpse of what he had just seen? Yet he had calmly announced that she wasn't his type!

Her fingers flew over the fastening of her skirt as she almost ripped it off, then dragged on the creased khaki trousers, tucking the folds of the matching shirt inside the waistband—but even that added bulk did little to hold them up. They slid down her slim hips, pooling around her ankles, totally impossible for her to wear.

'This won't work!' There was anger in her voice as she dragged the trousers up again and held them, but if Doyle heard it he gave no sign as he turned round. He shot an assessing look at her then dropped the bag he was carrying on to the ground and hunted through it until he found a length of heavy twine. Measuring an arm's length, he hacked it off, then walked across to where Gabrielle was standing, staring disgustedly down at the sagging trousers.

'Here, this will do the trick.' He reached out but she backed away from him at once, her grey eyes wary, and saw him smile as he held the twine out to her. 'Don't panic. I was just going to use this to secure those pants, nothing else.'

She flushed at his sarcasm, the colour running under her fine skin in a hot tide, and heard him laugh softly before he bent back to the task of threading the twine through the belt-loops on the trousers. When he had done that he tied the two ends in a sturdy knot, then stepped back. 'Won't win any fashion awards but it serves the purpose. Now, what about those shoes?'

Gabrielle bent to pick up the battered plimsolls, only then aware that she had been holding her breath. It had been strangely unsettling to have him perform such a task for her, even though his touch had been nothing but impersonal. Dropping down on to the ground, she slipped her feet into the shoes and laced them up as tightly as she could, forcing herself to push the incident to the back of her mind where it deserved to remain, but when Doyle suddenly spoke she couldn't help the sudden odd little lurch her pulse gave.

'How do they feel?'

She barely spared him a glance, afraid that he might somehow read her unease from her expression if she gave him half a chance, and that was something she had no intention of doing! 'Big, but I'll manage. It's just a shame that you left my case behind. I had other, far more suitable shoes in it.'

She had hoped to goad him but it rebounded on her as he picked up the rucksack and tossed it towards her with a mocking smile. 'And if you'd had a bit more practice at carrying your own things then you wouldn't be suffering now. So here, carry this, and look on it as a learning experience.'

He turned his back on her, slicing through the stem of a huge fern. Gabrielle stared down at the bag in fury. Just who did he think he was, treating her like a...a lackey? The temptation to leave the bag right there was great; it was only the thought of how Doyle might react when he discovered what she had done that stopped her.

She slipped the straps over her shoulders, settling the heavy bag as comfortably as she could on her back, then started after him, her eyes shooting daggers at his broad back while she ran through a list of names she would like to call him. Childish it might be, but it served the purpose of making her feel a whole lot better!

'We had better stop here.' Doyle's voice brought Gabrielle to a weary halt. Sighing, she eased the rucksack off her aching shoulders and flexed the stiff muscles, then sank down on to the ground.

It was late afternoon and her body was a mass of aches and pains, her muscles complaining bitterly at the strenuous exercise. Pushing a damp, straggly strand of hair out of her eyes, she glanced up at Doyle, and could have wept when she saw that he still looked little different from when they had set off. Oh, there were filthy marks on his shirt, a smudge or two on his face, but apart from that he looked as though this was part of an average working day! The man wasn't human if he could keep up this gruelling pace without any effect!

Leaning her head back against the rough bark of a tree, Gabrielle closed her eyes, not wanting to keep looking at such a paragon when she felt as though she'd been put through the wringer and squeezed out the other side. She had always prided herself on her fitness, making a point of working out at several expensive health clubs where she was a member in different parts of the world, but from the look of it all those fees had been sadly wasted!

'Come on. You can't lounge there. There's work to be done.'

Doyle's tone was curt, bringing her eyes open at once. She stared up at him and frowned.

'Work? What on earth are you talking about? It may have escaped your notice, mister, but we just happen to be stranded in the middle of a jungle—so what do you suggest I do? Call my broker to check on my shares?'

He smiled thinly, tossing the knife on to the ground so that it landed with its point buried in the earth just inches away from her feet. 'Oh, it hasn't escaped my notice, honey, but I rather think that you aren't fully aware of the situation we're in.' He glanced towards the heavy canopy of greenery which almost blotted out the light, then looked back at her.

'In about twenty minutes or so the heavens are going to open and unless we've managed to construct some kind of shelter by then we're going to get soaked. So up you get. Take the knife and cut down as many of those big shiny leaves as you can while I start fixing up some sort of a frame.'

Gabrielle stared at the quivering silver blade of the knife embedded in the ground, then back at Doyle, scarcely able to believe what she had heard. Did he honestly imagine that she was going to leap up and start hacking lumps out of the jungle when she was totally exhausted, just because *he* thought it was going to rain in twenty minutes' time?

'In a few minutes,' she said coolly. 'I'll just get my breath back first. It's not that I'm questioning your weather forecasting talents, but...'

She leant her head back against the tree again and closed her eyes, then opened them abruptly when she felt herself being hauled to her feet as hard hands clamped around her shoulders in a bruising grip. This close to him, Gabrielle could see the tiny white lines that fanned from the corners of his glittering eyes, see the darkness of stubble along his angular jaw, feel the heat radiating from his powerful body, and she swallowed hard, not liking the way her heart gave a shuddering little lurch before starting to beat rapidly.

'You would try the patience of a saint, lady. Has no one ever told you that?' He shook her, not hard, nor roughly, but with enough force to make her head loll on her slender neck before he set her from him and stared into her face. 'Now, we can either do this the easy way or the hard way; it's up to you. But whichever you choose, the outcome will be the same: you will move that pretty little backside off the ground and go and get those leaves cut. So... which is it to be?'

He folded his arms across his chest, staring at her with an arrogant tilt to his lips which made Gabrielle realise that he meant what he said. She looked away from those almost mesmerising eyes, wanting to refuse to do as he ordered. Only she had the feeling that it would be a mistake. She could only speculate about what he meant by doing things 'the hard way'!

She glared back at him, her chin tilted at a regal angle, hating to be forced into the position of backing down. 'If it's so important to you that I do it now, then I suppose I shall have to. But don't imagine that you can get away with treating me this way, Doyle. When we get back you could find yourself regretting your high-handed treatment of me!'

'*If* we get back, Gabby, *then* I shall worry about it, but until then I doubt I shall lose too much sleep.' He picked up the knife and handed it to her, then bent down and started to search through the rucksack, ignoring her completely as he pulled out several items and laid them on the ground.

Gabrielle watched him for a moment, then drew a sharp breath to ease the constriction in her chest caused by anger. She had never met anyone like him before! Didn't it matter to him that her family could buy and sell him a thousand times over? Apparently not!

She swung round, attacking the nearest towering fern with a vengeance, ruing the vagaries of a fate which had condemned her to spending time in the company of a man like him. When she thought of all the nice, charming men she could have been stranded with... Well!

She swung the knife at the thick stem, using every scrap of strength she possessed to cut it free from the springy trunk and tossing it on to the ground before wiping the perspiration out of her eyes with her sleeve as she glanced round at Doyle. He had his back to her, every muscle straining as he bent a young sapling over to form an arch then fastened it in place with a length of the twine. He worked swiftly as he tied more branches into place, every movement sure and economical, and Gabrielle frowned as a sudden, strangely unpalatable thought struck her.

Other men might treat her as she was accustomed to being treated, but which one of them could have coped if he'd been thrust into this situation? Could she really imagine Glen with his designer clothes soaked in perspiration as he worked like that? Or Robert—clever, witty, amusing Robert—even having the faintest idea what to do to get them to safety?

Gabrielle turned back to her task, hacking away as the pile of shiny dark green leaves grew while she ran through the names of every single one of the men in her wide circle of friends, men she had known and liked for years, yet who all suddenly seemed shallow and insubstantial. There wasn't one of them who could have risen to this challenge as Doyle had done. He had been rude, arrogant and completely overbearing, but if she'd had to be stranded with anyone then she was suddenly glad it was him! And the realisation shocked her rigid.

The rain started just as Doyle finished tying the last leaf in place. Gabrielle savoured the first cool drops on her hot skin but within seconds it had turned into a downpour, as though buckets of water were being tipped from the sky. She didn't need Doyle's curt order to get into the shelter. She scrambled beneath the archway, moving as far over as she could as Doyle followed her. There was barely room for them both but by drawing her legs under her Gabrielle managed to give him enough room to get in out of the downpour. She glanced up at the green canopy, which was proving to be surprisingly watertight so far.

'How did you know that it was going to rain like this now?'

'This is a rainforest,' he replied, then sighed when he saw her blank expression. 'It rains every day of the year here, at around four o'clock in the afternoon. You don't need to be a meteorologist to forecast it. It's been happening since the world began and will keep on happening until man and his greed destroys the cycle.'

There was a harsh edge to his deep voice and Gabrielle glanced warily at him before realising it wasn't aimed at her this time. 'You mean that if we keep on cutting down the trees then it could alter the weather pattern? It seems incredible, doesn't it?'

'What does seem incredible is that people are prepared to play around with something as important as this.' He took off his hat and tossed it on to the ground then finger-combed his thick dark hair back from his forehead. In the greenish gloom his face was all stark angles and planes, his expression hard to define. Only his eyes gave any indication of what he felt, pale and glittering in the dim light, filled with a weary kind of anger. 'Huge parts of the forest are being destroyed each day to build highways, to clear more space for farming, even just for the timber it yields. Yet if it carries on at this rate then experts estimate that the Amazon rainforest will have disappeared by the year 2020, and the effect on the world's climate can only be guessed at.'

'That's dreadful! Surely something can be done to stop such destruction?'

Doyle smiled thinly. 'What? You can't blame the government of Brazil for trying to improve their economy and give their poor land to grow food on. The country has been exploited for years and now it's time something was put back into it for the good of everyone, not just for the benefit of a few rich people who want to become even richer.'

Gabrielle stiffened, not slow to hear the note of condemnation in Doyle's voice. 'Why do I get the impression that that was aimed rather pointedly at me?'

'If the hat fits, Gabby.' He settled himself more comfortably on the spongy ground, one eyebrow raising mockingly as she moved quickly away an inch or two when his thigh brushed against her knee in the confined space.

She glared at him, hating the fact that she could feel heat surging under her skin. 'I don't see what I can do about this country's problems!'

'Perhaps not, but would you even try if there were something you could do? I mean, Gabby, how exactly do you fill your day from the time you get up to the time you go to bed? What do you give back to the world which has given you so much?'

'Stop calling me by that ridiculous name! I have already told you that I don't like it. And as for what I do... well, frankly I don't see that it is any of your business!'

'Perhaps not, but I must confess that it intrigues me. It can't be easy filling in your days with lunches, shopping, visits to the beauty salon. I mean, you appear to me to be an intelligent enough woman, so don't you find it all just a bit boring, day after day?'

His low voice mocked her, reminding her clearly of all her recent uncertainties about the life she led. He conjured up a shallow, aimless existence which was just too close to the truth, and Gabrielle resented the fact that he was making her feel so guilty. She stared haughtily back at him through the dim gloom, refusing to admit that she had been suffering her own doubts. She wouldn't give him the satisfaction of knowing that he had hit an increasingly raw nerve!

'Why should I dislike my life? I have everything I could possibly need or want.'

'Do you, indeed?' He smiled slowly, his eyes running over her from head to toe with an expression in them that made her want to shift uncomfortably. She curbed the urge and heard him laugh softly. 'You are a determined lady, Gabby. I'll say that for you. You don't like to admit that I'm right.'

She forced a smile. '*If* you had been right, Doyle, then I would have been adult enough to admit it, but I'm afraid you're way off the mark. There are an awful lot of people who would give anything to swap their life for mine, given the chance.'

'Perhaps, but I'm sure that a lot of them would be eager to swap back to a less privileged existence once they'd had a taste of it. How old are you?'

'I beg your pardon? What has my age got to do with you? In fact, what has anything about me and my lifestyle got to do with you?'

He shrugged lightly, his shirt straining across his chest, the movement drawing her eyes instantly to the powerful contours until she forced them away. 'I'm just making conversation. It's going to be a long few days if we don't speak to each other.'

It made a perverse kind of sense so Gabrielle bit back the hot retorts hovering on her tongue and tried to keep her tone just as level as his had been. 'I'm twenty-two. How old are you?'

He smiled narrowly. 'Thirty-four. Which makes me quite a bit older than you, and double that in experience, I imagine.'

She didn't like that faint mockery. 'While I can hardly claim to match your "experience", not knowing what it is, I am hardly the babe-in-arms you're trying to make me out to be. I have seen something of the world, Doyle!'

'And what you have seen has always been cushioned by your family's wealth, hasn't it? You have never really had to stand on your own two feet and make your own way in life.'

It was a criticism she couldn't refute, and she didn't attempt to try to do so, merely raising a slender brow in question. Doyle smiled, obviously unperturbed by her reaction. 'This is going to be a whole new experience for you, Gabby, isn't it? I mean, out here in this jungle there is no one to smooth your path, no one to lean on apart from yourself. For the first time in your life you're going to have to find out what sort of stuff you're made of.'

'And you don't think I shall manage it? Is that it?' She laughed out loud, relieved to understand suddenly what he was getting at. 'Well, if that was a challenge, then I accept. Whatever you can cope with, Doyle, I can too!'

'We shall see, I expect. Now, I suggest that you try to get some rest until the rain goes off. Once it's cleared up we shall be setting off again . . . as long as you think you're up to it?'

Gabrielle didn't bother to reply, turning away as she curled into a small ball, pillowed her head in her arms and closed her eyes. He was infuriating, so smugly confident that she wouldn't cope with whatever was to come! It was only as she was starting to drift into a light sleep that the thought struck her that maybe Doyle had been far cleverer than she had given him credit for. If she went to pieces, he would be put in the difficult position of trying to get both of them back to safety. But by issuing that challenge he knew that she would do her damnedest to keep up with him!

Why, of all the conniving, double-dealing, underhand ... She fell asleep before she could complete the full list of names she would have liked to call him!

CHAPTER THREE

THE pillow felt as though it had rocks in it!

Gabrielle eased her hand under her cheek to smooth the lumps out of the pillow, then froze when her fingers touched something which definitely wasn't her usual smooth satin bedding. Slowly, delicately, her fingers traced across the rough fabric, feeling the hardness beneath it, and she frowned in bewilderment. Her hand moved on until the roughness gave way to other textures—warm smoothness and a tantalising tickling sensation on her palm—and she smiled in sudden appreciation, letting her fingers enjoy the hard warm curves.

'Mmm, I think that's just about enough, honey. Otherwise I can't be held responsible for what happens next.' Strong fingers caught her wrist as a deep voice rumbled directly under her ear, and Gabrielle's sleepy eyes opened. For a moment she stared up into a pair of ice-blue eyes, wondering what was going on, and then comprehension returned with a vengeance.

With a tiny gasp of dismay she shot bolt upright, dragging her hand free of Doyle's grip, her face suffused with colour when she saw the way he was smiling at her. 'I... You... Damn it, Doyle, why didn't you wake me up?'

He gave a faint lift of one brow, then calmly buttoned the front of his shirt, mockery gleaming in his eyes when Gabrielle immediately averted her eyes from the naked

35

chest she had just been lying against and...stroking!
'What for? You obviously needed the rest and I can't
say that I objected to acting as your pillow, until things
started to get a trifle intimate.'

Her flush deepened, her cheeks burning with hot
colour as she recalled the way her hand had explored
those warm, hard muscles, savouring the texture of his
skin beneath that mat of dark, curling body hair. Sur-
reptitiously she rubbed her tingling palm down the side
of her leg to erase the lingering sensations, but it wasn't
that easy to remove them, it seemed. Annoyed and embarrassed, Gabrielle glared at him, her grey eyes stormy
with resentment. 'I had no idea that I was using you as
a pillow, but don't worry—it won't happen again. I shall
make sure of that!'

'Good. Now that you're finally awake I suggest we
make a start. We have a fair distance to cover so we
can't afford to waste time.' He dismissed her with a
galling ease, uncoiling his considerable length from the
makeshift shelter. Gabrielle counted to ten, took a deep
breath for good measure, and followed him, feigning
strategic blindness when he offered her a hand to help
her to her feet. Frankly she'd had quite enough of
touching him to last her for today—and for a few days
to come!

Ignoring Doyle completely, she stretched her cramped
muscles and took a look round in the vain hope that
their situation might have changed, but it hadn't. There
was still that all-encompassing wall of green sur-
rounding them, the only difference now being that it was
a lot darker than it had been before, the air even more
laden with moisture. Even doing nothing more strenuous
than standing up she could feel perspiration coating her

body, running down between her breasts and soaking into the back of her shirt.

'Here. We'd better have something to eat before we set off again.' Doyle handed her a foil-wrapped package and Gabrielle stared down at it curiously for a moment before peeling it open and studying the unappetising-looking biscuit it contained with dismay.

'It looks revolting!'

He ignored her tone, biting into the biscuit he held with strong white teeth and chewing the mouthful before answering. 'If it's any consolation then I can assure you that that biscuit contains everything you need in the way of vitamins and minerals.' He took another bite and chewed it slowly, watching Gabrielle as she took a hesitant nibble then gave a small grimace. 'Of course if you really don't want it then there is always what Mother Nature provides from her store-cupboard.'

There was a note in his voice which should have warned her not to ask, but her senses were still somewhat be-fuddled from the shock of wakening. 'And what is that? Although I'm sure it can't be much worse than this.'

'Monkey, snake, lizard. I believe they are particularly tasty if you can catch young ones.'

Gabrielle glared into his mocking face. 'Oh, ha ha, very funny! Thank you, but I think I shall stick to this after all. It appears to be the best thing on offer.'

'What did you expect, Gabby? Silver service right here in the middle of the jungle?' There was cool contempt in his deep voice and it stung.

'No, I did not! Why don't you stop trying to poke fun at me, Doyle? I haven't done anything at all to you! So back off!'

'Delighted to, just so long as you realise that this isn't going to be any picnic, lady. We have a long, hard trek ahead of us. Understand?'

'Perfectly.' She chewed and swallowed the rest of the dry biscuit, forcing herself to finish every crumb, then stared defiantly at him. 'I'm ready when you are.'

He merely nodded, moving ahead of her as he took a bearing from the compass set into the handle of his knife before starting to hack away at the wall of plants. Gabrielle started after him, then paused when she saw the rucksack lying on the ground. With a heavy sigh and a venomous look at Doyle's back she went and picked it up, settling it on to her shoulders as she followed him into the trees.

He might think he had the upper hand right now but once they got back to civilisation all that would change. She was going to make him pay for every single thing he had said and done to taunt her! She could put up with a lot with that thought to keep her going.

It was almost dark when they finally stopped for the night. Gabrielle had been going on automatic pilot for the past laborious mile, so that when Doyle came to a halt she almost ran into the back of him. She stood swaying on her feet, toying with the tempting idea of just dropping down where she stood and sleeping for a week. But obviously Doyle had no intention of allowing her such luxury.

Easing the rucksack off her shoulders, he set it down on the ground and produced a torch from the pocket, switching it on so that the beam cast an eerie glow around the small clearing they had discovered in the middle of the trees. Gabrielle watched in silence as he delved into the bag then drew out a tin cup and handed it to her.

'Take this and see if you can fill it with water.'

Gabrielle stared at it blankly then looked around the clearing before turning back to Doyle who was now taking other mysterious items out of the bag. 'Where am I going to find water? Is there a stream around here or something?'

He gave an impatient sigh, uncoiling his considerable length from his cramped position to take the cup back from her. 'The "or something" is about right. Here, follow me, and I'll demonstrate the mysteries of jungle plumbing.'

Gabrielle wasn't sure she liked his tone but it seemed easier to say nothing rather than start a quarrel when she was feeling so exhausted. Without a word she followed him to the edge of the trees, watching wide-eyed while he pulled a curling leaf downwards so that a stream of rainwater ran into the cup. He shot her a quick glance, then handed her back the cup. 'Right, get the idea now? Think you can manage it?'

He turned to walk back across the clearing but suddenly, tired or not, Gabrielle refused to let him get away with taunting her like that. She caught his arm, her fingers closing around the hard muscles as she brought him to a halt, and glared into his arrogant face with anger in her eyes. 'You don't miss any opportunity, do you, mister? What is it with you? Is your ego so fragile that you need to boost it up all the time by showing how clever you are?'

He swung round to face her, his pale eyes dropping to where her hand was still holding his arm and, despite herself, Gabrielle let it drop to her side and took a hasty step back. 'My ego is fine, Gabby. It doesn't need boosting. Why should it? I don't give a damn what you think of me. All I care about is getting us out of this mess we're in, but if you want to delude yourself then be my guest. Now, if you're sure that you can handle it, I shall go and get the stove working.' He cast an assessing glance round the small clearing, which looked dim and shadowy in the pitiful light cast by the torch. 'In another half-hour or so this place is going to be as dark as Hades, so I suggest you get a move on otherwise dinner will be a repeat of lunch, and I'm sure that won't meet with your ladyship's approval.' He laughed but there was no amusement in the sound, just a cold, chilling contempt which made Gabrielle shiver despite the steamy heat. 'This little jaunt is going to be really rough on your delicate palate, isn't it, Gabby?'

There he went again, mocking her, taunting her, making fun of her! Gabrielle rounded on him in fury. 'It won't be any rougher on me than it is on you!'

'Think not?' He caught her suddenly, pulling her towards him so fast that she slammed against his chest and would have fallen if he hadn't retained a grip on her waist. He caught her hand, lifting it up to turn it over and study the smooth palm, the manicured nails. Slowly he stroked the pad of his thumb over the soft flesh, smiling when he felt the roughness of his own hand in such a startling contrast to hers. When Gabrielle dragged her hand away he let it go, but instead hooked a finger under her chin and tilted her face into the soft beam of light while he traced the pale, fine skin, the delicate bones beneath. Gabrielle could feel her heart skip a beat and she bit her lip hard, concentrating on that pain to keep her mind away from the strange sensations which were flowing through her as she stood there in Doyle's arms.

'You're a beautiful woman, Gabby, but you don't need me to tell you that, I'm sure. You must see it yourself each time you look in the mirror, see how soft your skin is, just like satin, and so fine that it's virtually translucent. But why shouldn't it be? You have all the time and the money to keep your skin soft, your hair silky, to *pamper* your beauty. You've led a cushioned life and nothing in it has prepared you for how rough these next few days might be. I would be doing you a huge disservice by allowing you to expect anything else!'

Gabrielle twisted her head away from his hand, glaring up at him so that he would see how much she loathed him, and not see how she felt about being held this way. 'Perhaps I don't have much idea of what we might have to face but is it my fault that I haven't been in this situation before? I can't help being who I am, nor can I help how I live, yet you make it sound like some sort of a crime! You won't even give me a chance, Doyle, will you? And I don't really understand why not!'

Something glittered in his pale eyes and his hands tightened so that Gabrielle gasped in pain, yet she knew that he wasn't even aware of inflicting it. Then abruptly he let her go, turning away to walk back to the rucksack and crouch down by it, no expression on his face now as he said curtly, 'If we're to get anything to eat before it gets dark you'd better get a move on with that water.'

Gabrielle took a shaky little breath, more disturbed by what had happened than she wanted to admit. Had she imagined that fleeting expression on Doyle's face just now, that raw, bitter flash of pain? She glanced across at where he was crouched, studied the strong, clean lines of his profile, and knew it hadn't been imagination. Something had happened in Doyle's past, something which in some odd way affected how he behaved with her, and suddenly she longed to know what it was.

Picking up the tin mug from where it had dropped on the ground during their disagreement, she walked to the trees and started to fill it with rainwater, trying hard to push the incident to the back of her mind where it deserved to remain. If Doyle had some sort of hang-up then that was his problem; it shouldn't worry her one bit, but it did. She, Gabrielle Marshall, who had never in her life cared what anyone thought of her, suddenly wanted this man, this rude, arrogant, impossible stranger, to like her!

The soup tasted like nectar. Gabrielle took a last, slowly appreciative sip then handed the mug to Doyle, watching as he drained the last drop from it. He set it down then glanced across at her. He had left the small stove burning and in the flickering blue-gold flame his face looked stern and remote, his expression unreadable. Gabrielle shifted uncomfortably, glancing down at her hands while she examined the smooth oval nails as though she found the sight of them entrancing. They'd hardly exchanged a word since they had sat down to eat the soup Doyle had made from mixing the rainwater with one of the packets he had in the rucksack. Now the air between them seemed to be charged with a kind of tension she found impossible to break. It was only when Doyle suddenly got up and started towards the trees that she forced herself to speak.

'Where are you going?'

There was a trace of alarm in her voice and he stopped at once to glance back at her with a faint lift of one dark brow before replying evenly, 'I won't be long. Don't worry.'

Gabrielle flushed as comprehension dawned. Picking up the mug, she got up and carried it over to the other side of the clearing to wash out the soupy dregs, then shook it dry. Walking back to where the rucksack was lying next to the stove, she packed the tin mug away, smiling wryly as she did so. Her mother would never believe it if she could see her now, clearing up!

'What's so funny?'

She jumped as Doyle suddenly appeared, and stepped back so that her foot caught against the small stove.

'Careful!' With lightning reactions he leapt forward, drawing her away from the flickering flame which was licking at the bottom of her trouser-leg. 'Dammit, lady, don't you know better than to be so careless around a naked flame?' he bit out.

Gabrielle glared at him, feeling her heart beating rapidly with fright and some other emotion she had no intention of trying to identify. She dragged herself away from his disturbing hold, her grey eyes stormy. 'If you hadn't come pussy-footing up then it would never have happened!'

For a moment he seemed about to reply just as hotly, then obviously controlled the urge, his pale eyes indifferent as he cast her one last glance before bending to attend to the stove which was half lying on its side. 'We'd better get some sleep. We need to set off as soon as it's light.'

Gabrielle glanced round the small clearing, forcing herself to match his even tone. 'Are we going to have to build another shelter?'

He shook his head, his dark brown hair catching the glow from the firelight so that for a moment he seemed to be surrounded by a golden halo. 'No point. It won't rain so it makes no difference whether we sleep under cover or out in the open.' He pointed to the ground by the stove. 'Here will be as good a place as any. I suggest you button that shirt up as tight as it will go and tie the bottoms of your trouser legs with some of that twine. That way you should be able to keep away most of the insects.'

Gabrielle shuddered at the thought, but said nothing as she hunted in the rucksack for the twine and cut off a couple of lengths before glancing over at Doyle, who even now was making himself comfortable on the ground. 'Do you want some of this?' she asked, holding the ball up for him to see, but he shook his head before calmly tipping his hat over his eyes.

Gabrielle glared at his relaxed figure, wishing she could feel so at ease. Did nothing ever dent that composure of his? Seemingly not. It took a few minutes to fasten the bottoms of the trousers securely and button up the shirt but even then she was loath to lie down on the ground. It was the thought of all those insects waiting there, ready to crawl all over her the moment she relaxed!

'You can't stay awake all night long, Gabby. You need to sleep.'

'I'm fine! Don't concern yourself about me. I...I'm not tired just yet.'

'No?' He tipped his hat back on his head, watching her through slitted eyes which, even in the poor light, she could see held more than a glint of knowing mockery. 'From where I'm lying, lady, you look out on your feet.'

'Well, you're wrong. I feel fine—marvellous, in fact. I shall just sit here for a while and...and...' She tailed off, unable to find some reason for not taking the sensible course of action. Although she hated to admit it,

Doyle was right about her needing to get some sleep. The day's trek had drained her and she needed sleep to restore her energy, but how could she sleep with the thought of what might be going on beneath her, all those creepy-crawly insects just lying in wait for her?

'Enjoy the view?' he suggested helpfully. He sat up, reaching over to the small stove. 'Sorry, Gabby. I hate to spoil your night but I'm afraid I shall have to turn this off. We can't afford to waste what resources we have.'

He flicked the switch on the stove, watching patiently as the flame spluttered then slowly faded into nothing, leaving them in total darkness. Gabrielle drew in a sharp breath, feeling every nerve in her body reacting with an almost primeval instinct to the absence of light, so that her skin prickled. From a few feet away she heard a soft rustling as Doyle made himself comfortable again but to her suddenly painfully attuned hearing the sound seemed unnaturally loud, as though there wasn't just him moving around. She drew herself into a tight little ball, huddling her knees to her chest, trying to make herself as small as possible in the darkness which seemed to press in on her from all sides like something tangible.

'You can always come over here and lie next to me if you're scared.'

Doyle's voice was deep and soft, strangely alluring as it floated from the dark void, and Gabrielle bit her lip as fear and pride warred. It was tempting to do as he suggested but... 'No, thanks. I'm fine,' she answered quickly, before she could change her mind.

'Suit yourself. Pleasant dreams, Gabby.'

There was another soft rustling, then silence. Gabrielle's ears strained against it as she tried to hear

Doyle's breathing, just to reassure herself that he was still there, but the harder she listened, the more strange sounds she could hear—sounds that she couldn't identify but which her mind went spinning off to make sense of.

Was that soft, slithering sound a snake moving across the ground towards her? And that light, insistent tapping—could it be...? The shrill shriek which cut through all the other noises brought her to her feet with a cry of alarm as she prepared to run from whatever horror was approaching, but she got no further than a couple of steps before strong arms fastened around her legs and brought her tumbling to the ground.

'For heaven's sake!' There was rough impatience in Doyle's deep voice, but surprisingly the hands which held her when she struggled wildly were gentle, firm and strangely reassuring. He drew her closer, pinning her to the ground with his muscular torso, forcing her to listen to what he was trying to tell her. 'It was just a monkey, Gabby. It won't hurt you. You probably scared it half to death screaming the way you did.'

Gabrielle sucked in a lungful of air as she tried to get her fear under control again, and found it was easier than she would have thought. She could feel the solid strength of Doyle's muscular chest against her breasts, feel the steady beat of his heart taming hers to an easier rhythm, hear the soft sound of his breathing blotting out all the other unfamiliar sounds in the night, and the fear gradually faded.

He must have felt the tension flowing out of her because he relaxed his hold, although he made no attempt to move away from her. Under the thin, slightly damp cotton of his shirt his skin burned, the heat flowing from his big body into hers, touching her with an answering heat which owed little to the jungle conditions. Gabrielle could feel it stealing along her limbs, pouring through her veins like warm, honeyed wine, making her feel oddly languorous. When he suddenly drew away her hand half raised to stop him before she suddenly realised what she was doing. She let it drop to her side, glad of the darkness now because it hid her embarrassment from his eyes.

'Right, if you're sure you aren't going to go rushing off again, shall we try to get some sleep?' Doyle's voice was once more cool, faintly cutting, holding the usual note of indifference she had come to expect when he spoke to her, and Gabrielle answered in similar vein.

'I'm fine. I apologise for disturbing you.' She lay down on the ground, settling herself as comfortably as she could against the lumps and bumps, and closed her eyes, listening as Doyle settled down beside her. His arm brushed hers and Gabrielle moved away so that there would be no chance of their bodies touching again, uncaring what he thought of her actions. He could put any interpretation he liked on it. All she knew was that there was no way she was going to risk being beset by that crazy fever she'd felt before when he had held her. She had no idea what had caused such a reaction but something warned her that it would be dangerous to allow it to happen again.

She rolled over, setting another few valuable inches of space between their bodies as she stared up at the pitch-black canopy of leaves and listened to Doyle's steady breathing as he fell asleep. Only then did she deem it safe to allow her own weary body to let sleep claim it—safe for now, at least, from that unexpected touch of jungle fever!

CHAPTER FOUR

THERE was no sign of Doyle when Gabrielle awoke the next morning. For a moment she lay still, staring round the small clearing through the mist which was rising from the trees, while she tried to shake off the lingering remnants of half remembered yet oddly disturbing dreams. Then with a low groan she pushed her stiff muscles into action and started to scramble to her feet, just as Doyle suddenly appeared out of the jungle.

For a moment which bordered on eternity Gabrielle's widening eyes rested on him, drinking in the sight he made backdropped against the greenery. Dressed only in dark boxer shorts which sat low on his narrow hips, with his broad chest bare and gleaming with droplets of water, he looked magnificently pagan, his muscular body honed to perfection. Gabrielle dropped her eyes, struggling the rest of the way to her feet as she fought against the rising tide of heat she could feel flowing through her. Doyle was wearing no more and no less than any man might wear on the beach—so why did her pulse feel as though it was going to explode, her heart feel as though it would burst to win the race it was obviously running.

Deliberately she turned her back on him, then jumped when he tossed a bundle of clothing on to the ground near her feet before crouching down beside the stove to light it. 'There's a stream and a pool through the trees over there. The water is cold but it feels good to wash some of the dirt off. I'll make some coffee if you want to try it for yourself.'

'I...it sounds like a good idea.' Gabrielle nodded, her eyes barely skimming over him before she turned away and heard him laugh harshly.

'Sorry, Gabby. I quite forgot about your delicate and highly refined sensibilities.'

She stopped at once, her stomach lurching at the thought that he might have realised how unnerved she'd felt at seeing him like this. 'I have no idea what you mean,' she said stiffly.

He rolled to his feet, uncoiling his long legs from under him as he walked over to where she was standing and bent to smile at her. This close she could smell the clean scent of his skin, see the smoothness of the flesh over the hard muscles in his arms and the whorling pattern of hair on his chest before it arrowed down to disappear beneath the waistband of his shorts, and the breath seemed to catch in her lungs, making any further speech impossible.

'I forgot that a woman like you would find it distasteful suddenly to find a half-naked man parading around. I apologise for my social gaffe.'

His words mocked her, his tone little short of insulting, but Gabrielle found it impossible to reply. She swung away from him, pushing through the undergrowth in the direction he had indicated while she called herself every sort of fool for letting him affect her this way. Why should she find the sight of him so disturbing when she had never felt like that before over any man? As she had grown older and had still never met a man who had aroused anything approaching desire in her, she had started to wonder if there was something wrong with her. All her friends seemed to fall in and out of love, and in and out of bed with each other, yet Gabrielle had remained aloof from that kind of behaviour, something inside her shying away from accepting second-best. She had never met a man she had really wanted in that way, yet there was no denying that what she had felt just now when she'd seen Doyle had been desire, pure and simple and totally inexplicable!

The thought kept her company as she made her way through the trees until she suddenly arrived at the pool. She stared round, hardly able to believe that this small part of paradise could exist in the middle of the steamy jungle. The silvery trickle of the waterfall, which fell from the rocks to drop into the shallow basin below it, was perfect, like something out of a painting. Exotic tropical plants flowered all around the pool, their brilliant colours repeated in the plumage of the birds which dipped and flew overhead. Gabrielle watched as a pair of red-crested birds landed on a tree near by before swooping down to the pool, their wings setting tiny ripples across its glassy surface. The whole place was an oasis of beauty in the unrelenting harshness of the jungle and she could have stayed there for ages, just enjoying it, but time—and Doyle—would wait for no man!

With a sigh, Gabrielle stripped off her clothes, only hesitating briefly about removing her underwear. There was no one about to see her if she went in naked and the thought of being able to shed the clammy clothing at last was too tempting to resist. Leaving the bundle of clothes on a flat rock at the edge of the pool, she slid into the water and gasped at its coldness. It felt icy after the steamy heat among the trees and her skin puckered into goose-pimples until gradually she adjusted to the change in temperature.

Ducking under the water, Gabrielle washed her hair, then pushed it back from her face as she started to swim to the other side of the pool where the waterfall cascaded into it. It was deliciously refreshing under the cool spray of water, like a very special sort of shower, and she let herself drift in and out, catching the silvery drops in her hands before letting them slide between her fingers.

'I hate to be the one to spoil your fun, Gabby, but we don't have all day to spare while you play mermaid.'

The unexpected sound of Doyle's voice startled her so much that she sank like a stone, and came rushing back to the surface spluttering water. Dragging the wet strands of hair out of her eyes, she stared across the pool and saw him standing on the opposite side, hands on hips, legs apart as he glared at her with impatient silver-blue eyes. For a moment Gabrielle glared back, then suddenly realised that she was in no position to be fighting silent battles in her state of undress.

She sank beneath the clear water, going hot and cold when she imagined what he must have seen of her slender body. 'Do you mind?' she snapped. 'I should have thought that common decency would demand that you afford me some privacy.'

His mouth curled. 'I'm afraid you've used up all the privacy allowance you're entitled to for today. Hurry it up. We need to get started.'

He turned to walk away back through the trees, obviously viewing that as the end to the conversation which, rationally, it should have been. So why did Gabrielle hear herself saying with a feeling of total disbelief, 'I'll be out when I'm good and ready and not before.'?

Doyle paused in mid-stride, his face unreadable as he glanced back at her. 'I beg your pardon?'

A shiver slid down her spine at his tone but she ignored it, some little voice inside her head urging her on. 'I think you heard me.'

He walked back to the pool and stopped on the bank, his pale eyes glittering as silvery as the cascading water. 'Oh, I heard all right, Gabby. I was just having a bit of trouble believing it.'

She smiled sweetly, scooping up a handful of water to skim it across the surface so that a few drops landed on his boots. 'I don't see why there should be a problem. I've told you that I shall be out as soon as I am ready, so...'

'So you expect me to hang around waiting for you. Is that right?' He crouched down, his forearms resting on his muscular thighs as he balanced on the balls of his feet. Gabrielle had the sudden uneasy feeling that she was seeing a sleek tiger watching its prey before making up its mind when to pounce, but curbed the fanciful idea. Doyle had done nothing but make life difficult for her since they had met, so why shouldn't she ruffle his fur up the wrong way for a change?

She held back a giggle at the simile, smiling calmly back at him. 'Of course. You can hardly leave without me, can you?'

He seemed to consider that statement for a trifle longer than was perhaps strictly necessary before suddenly straightening up. 'It's open to debate, I expect. But no, I imagine that you have already worked out that I won't actually leave you behind, even though the idea holds a certain temptation.'

Gabrielle wasn't sure she liked the tone in his deep voice. It made the back of her neck prickle although she couldn't have explained why. She watched warily as Doyle moved a few feet away from the edge of the pool then bent down to unlace his boots. 'What...what are you doing?'

He didn't bother to answer, calmly taking the boots off and standing them neatly side by side next to her own bundle of clothing before he started to unbutton his shirt.

'Doyle!'

He glanced over at where she was huddled in the water, smiling calmly as he tossed the shirt on to the pile then unzipped his trousers and tossed them after it. 'I'm not quite sure what sort of game you're playing, Gabby, but I'm willing to find out.'

'Game? I'm not playing any... Doyle!' Her voice rose to a shriek as he slid into the water and swam strongly across to where she was trying to keep afloat yet keep herself hidden beneath the surface. Standing up, he shook water off his face and smiled down at her in a way which sent a shimmer of excitement racing down her spine, even though she hated herself for feeling that way.

'This little game of enticement. That's what it is, isn't it, sweet? You want to see if I'm just as susceptible to your charms as all the other men you meet?'

'I... No! You have it all wrong. I wasn't... I didn't... Damn you, Doyle, I was not trying to seduce you!' She half rose from the water then sank back when she saw his eyes drop to her bare breasts. The cold water had made her nipples pucker and under the steady scrutiny of his silvery gaze she could feel them starting to throb.

Colour flowed into her cheeks and she turned her head
so that she couldn't see what he was thinking, but he
calmly hooked his hand behind her head and turned it
back.

'Weren't you, Gabrielle? Are you sure? Isn't that really
why you started this provocative little game?'

His voice was slow and deep, sending shivers of reaction down her spine as it flowed through the silence
between them. Gabrielle shook her head, feeling his
fingers sliding through the damp silk of her hair to press
against her scalp in a touch which was both intimate and
seductive. 'No.'

'It's understandable, really. You've been thrust into a
situation way beyond anything you've encountered
before. It's all new and strange, isn't it, Gabby? You
aren't sure you can cope, so you instigate a situation
where you can be in control—a tried and tested way of
re-asserting yourself. And I have to confess it isn't hard
to play this game with you, honey.'

His voice dropped an octave, dark and delicious, like
brown velvet as it stroked her senses, just an instant
before he drew her closer so that her body brushed
against his, bare skin smoothing against bare skin.
Gabrielle gasped at the feel of Doyle's hard body against
hers, unprepared for the shock which ran through her
as every nerve-ending responded to a new kind of
stimulus, and heard him murmur something harsh before
his head came down and he took her mouth in a kiss
which seemed to draw all the strength from her. His lips
were hot and demanding as they moved over hers—such
a contrast to the coolness of their water-chilled flesh that
she instinctively sought the heat and moved closer
to him.

The pool must have deepened at that point because suddenly there was nothing beneath her feet except water, but Doyle wrapped his arm around the back of her waist, holding her against his powerful body as he kept her afloat, and moved his mouth along the curve of her jaw, around the delicate shell of her ear then on to her temple, leaving behind a trail of fire. When his hands slid down her spine, to mould her against him, Gabrielle made no move to stop him, enthralled by the spell of sensation he was casting over her. She could feel every hard, powerful inch of his body, feel the muscles rippling under her fingers as she slid her hands up to his shoulders and braced herself against the slight tug of the water, and something inside her reacted to it in a way as old as time—woman responding to man.

'Doyle, I...'

His hands tightened around her, holding her so close that she seemed to merge with him, skin to skin, flesh to flesh. Then almost roughly he moved her away, his hands strangely impersonal now as he held her afloat in the water. 'Well, has that done the trick, Gabby?'

'I...I don't understand what you're talking about.' What she had been about to say faded from her mind, her eyes filling with confusion as they met his cool ones and tried to follow what was happening. A moment ago they had been as close as a man and a woman could get without actual intimacy, yet now Doyle was looking at her almost as though she were a stranger!

'Reassured you, honey?' He smiled coolly, his eyes skimming below the surface of the water in a long, assessing look which brought the heat into her cheeks even while her body seemed to go cold. 'You haven't lost any of your allure, Gabby. You make any man want to possess you—so does that help? Will you be able to cope with what is to come knowing that at least that aspect of your life hasn't altered?'

'I . . .' She couldn't find the words. They seemed to be lost in some painful cavernous place deep inside her, held there by a pain which seemed to be ripping her heart to shreds. This had all been some sort of *exercise* to him! Planned and executed with a total lack of feeling which made a mockery of all those hot, sweet kisses he had given her.

It was pride which finally gave her the strength not to fall apart in front of him, and pride which made her tilt her head back and smile at him with a semblance of self-assurance. 'Mmm, yes, you're right, of course. I did need a little boost and it's always good to know that you're still in control of at least a part of your life. Thank you, Doyle.'

Her tone was a dismissal, telling him that he had served his purpose and that was the end of his usefulness as far as she was concerned. But if she had meant to goad him by it she was doomed to disappointment as he merely nodded and turned around to swim back across the pool.

Gabrielle waited until he had picked up his clothes and disappeared again into the trees before following him across to the bank and hauling herself wearily out of the water. Picking up her clothes, she dragged them on, uncaring that her wet body soaked them in seconds. Bending over, she wrung the water out of her long hair, watching the tiny droplets dropping into the moss, and if they were joined by other salty droplets from her eyes then she pretended not to see them. Doyle had taught her a valuable lesson today and she wouldn't cry. She wouldn't give him the satisfaction of guessing how much he had hurt her. To let him know how oddly vulnerable she was to him would be a mistake.

The day was almost a replay of the first. Gabrielle had long since lost any sense of direction as they made a path through the encompassing jungle. She had no idea if Doyle was leading them in the right direction or not and frankly couldn't have cared. It was too much effort to worry about that when it demanded all her strength and determination just to keep up with him.

They made another rough shelter just before it started to rain again. Gabrielle crawled inside, almost too exhausted to draw her legs beneath her so that Doyle could fit in too. He'd hardly said a word to her since he'd left her at the pool and she had made no attempt to break the silence. She was afraid that anything she might say would be too much, that the aching, nagging pain would loosen her tongue to emit words she could only regret. Once this was all over and they were safely back in civilisation she could forget what had happened and put Doyle out of her mind for good, but right now that was impossible when every time she looked up there he was, his powerful body pushing a way through the jungle, muscles rippling in his arms and shoulders as he wielded the knife to cut through the trees.

Gabrielle closed her eyes to blank out the picture but that didn't help because it merely seemed to bring it into sharper focus. She fell into an exhausted sleep with the image imprinted in her mind, and awoke some time later to find Doyle shaking her gently. For a moment she stared up into his face as the image merged with reality, then abruptly sat up so that his hand fell from her arm.

'Is it time to set off again?' she asked huskily as she ran a hand through her tangled hair to push it back from her damp face. Her heart was beating rapidly yet she felt almost dizzy, as though there was little blood getting through to her head, and instantly attributed it to the shock of being woken up so suddenly, afraid to look any further for its cause.

Doyle shook his head, studying her closely for a brief moment before he picked up the tin mug and offered it to her. 'We won't go any further today. Drink this. It will do you good.'

He handed Gabrielle the mug, watching silently as she took a sip of the soup. She offered it to him, feeling a strange little shudder work its way through every cell when he smiled. He had never smiled at her that way before. Always there had been mockery in the curve of his chiselled lips, a silent taunt, but now all they held was a warmth which made her feel almost breathless. She glanced down at the mug, tipping the soup from side to side while she tried to work out how one smile could make her feel like shouting for joy, then realised that she had missed his reply.

'I . . . I'm sorry. What did you say?'

He crouched down beside her, settling back on his heels as he tapped the mug with a long finger. 'I said that I'd already had some while you were asleep. So go on, Gabby, get it all drunk.'

Gabrielle took another sip of the hot liquid then glanced at him, her eyes skittering away before they could make contact with that disturbing silver-blue gaze. 'You should have woken me up sooner. Can we afford the time to stop for the rest of the day?'

Doyle shrugged as he took off his battered hat and tossed it on to the ground. 'There's no point in pushing ourselves too hard. It won't achieve anything if we end up too exhausted to make the last couple of miles.'

And for 'we' read 'you'! Gabrielle thought. She stiffened, glaring back at him as she set the mug down on the ground. 'If you are implying that *I* need to rest because I can't keep up the pace you're setting then let me tell you, mister, that you are sadly mistaken! Anything you can do I can do too!'

'Anything?' There was a note in his voice which brought her eyes to his at once and she felt herself grow hot at the expression she saw there. 'I imagine there are one or two things you can't do, Gabby—one or two *differences* between us. I think we discovered that only too well earlier today, and very enjoyable it was too.'

'Enjoyable? If it was so damned *enjoyable* then why did you s——?' She clamped a hand over her mouth but it was impossible to take back what she'd been about to say. She stared at Doyle in horror, watching the way a nerve pulsed heavily along his jaw.

'Why did I stop? Why do you think?' His eyes were glacial, his face hard with anger. 'This is going to be bad enough to contend with without allowing the situation between us to develop into something more.' He laughed harshly, sweeping her with a contemptuous look. 'Perhaps I was a bit slow this morning, lady. Perhaps there was more behind that little episode in the pool than I realised.'

'I have no idea what you are talking about and, frankly, no interest in finding out what it is!' She raised the mug to her lips, her hand shaking, so that soup slopped on to the front of her shirt. Doyle reached out and wiped it away with a lean finger, then calmly took the mug from her and set it down on the ground.

'Careful, Gabby. We don't want you scalding that delectable body, do we? Although I don't see why you should be feeling so embarrassed. Sexual appetites are just as strong as any other and need feeding. But unfortunately, for the days we are forced to stay together, you will have to starve—although I have to confess it wouldn't be any hardship to oblige you in that direction.' His eyes dropped to the soft swell of her breasts under the damp khaki and lingered for a second before lifting back to tangle with hers. 'Of course, if you still feel the same kind of urge once we're back in civilisation...'

'Why, you...you...' Gabrielle fought for words, but it was impossible to find anything suitable so she settled for actions instead. Her hand arced through the air but before it could make contact with Doyle's lean cheek his hand clamped over her wrist, his fingers bruising as they tightened around the fragile bones. Gabrielle winced, glaring up at him through eyes misted with tears of pain. 'I hate you, Doyle! You are totally despicable, and if you imagine for a second that I'm interested in...in making love with you then you're sadly mistaken!'

He drew her to him, his expression inscrutable as he stared into her angry face. 'I don't recall making any mention of love, Gabby. I was talking about sex, but perhaps you prefer to dress your affairs up in the guise of respectability.' He laughed suddenly, tipping her chin up so that he could search her eyes, and she went cold at the taunting light she could see in his glittering silver gaze. 'Is that what you tell yourself each time you take a new lover—that you're in love with him? How convenient to be able to excuse your basic appetites in such a way!'

'I don't have any——' She stopped abruptly, suddenly realising what she'd been about to say—every revealing word. Her face flamed with embarrassment and she looked away, terrified that he might guess somehow. But she should have realised that Doyle would always believe the worst of her.

He thrust her away from him, contempt lying coldly on his face. 'You don't have any need to make excuses to me? Is that what you were about to say before you thought better of it, honey? Well, at least it's good to know you're prepared to be honest sometimes. And you're quite right, of course. The way you lead your life is none of my business normally, but while we're stuck here together we may as well get the ground rules straight. I won't be used as a convenience for you, Gabby, not in any way at all. Understand?'

She understood all right, only too clearly, and her temper flared at his arrogance. 'Perfectly! But let *me* make it clear that it cuts two ways, Doyle.' She slid her gaze over him in a look which was little short of an insult, tilting her head to the side so that the heavy waves of chestnut hair spilled over her shoulder. 'If you have any urges which need satisfying then don't make the mistake of imagining that I shall be happy to oblige. You're not really my type, I'm afraid, Doyle. I like men to have a bit more...finesse than you seem capable of.'

'Is that so?' With a speed which shocked her he had her in his arms, holding her so tightly that despite her frantic struggles she couldn't free herself.

'Let me go!' Desperately Gabrielle twisted and turned in his encircling arms, but it was a battle she was destined to lose as Doyle simply held her until she was exhausted from the effort.

When she lay panting against him he smiled gently, but there was no sign of gentleness in his eyes, just a grim determination to make her bend to his will. 'So I leave you cold, do I, Gabby? My lack of finesse is a turn-off?'

'Yes!' She spat the reply back at him and knew at once that it was a mistake.

Weaving his fingers through the heavy strands of her hair, he forced her head back so that he could brush her mouth with his, letting his lips barely touch hers before they moved away, only to return and touch them again in a rhythm which made her tremble. He smiled when he felt her reaction, his pale eyes studying her for a moment. 'How am I doing, Gabby? Is my technique improving, or do I need to refine it some more?'

'Yes...I mean, no. Stop it, Doyle!' She turned her head, then winced at the painful tug on the roots of her hair, but it was better to endure the discomfort rather than the alternative. Determinedly she kept her face averted from him, then felt her heart jump when she felt his mouth against the cord of her neck, felt the tip of his tongue tracing the delicate ridge from her throat to her jaw. Heat flowed along her veins in a sudden wild frenzy which she only just managed to control, spurred on by the thought of Doyle's amusement if he realised how devastatingly potent she found his caresses. But when she felt the soft bite of his teeth on the lobe of her ear she couldn't help the shudder which rippled through her, and knew at once that he had felt it.

He drew back, turning her face to his, his hand insistent so that Gabrielle was unable to avoid doing as he wanted. 'I can make you want me, Gabby. We both know that.' He shrugged, his chest brushing against her aching breasts, and she tried to draw away from him, aware of the hardness of her nipples—such a betraying sign that Doyle was right. He glanced down then up, watching the colour fade from her face when she saw the awareness in his eyes. 'You can try to lie all you like, sweet, but it won't change anything. You might not consider my performance up to your usual standards, the same as I might find your morals sadly wanting, but that's our minds talking. Our bodies speak an entirely different language.'

He let her go, setting some space between them so that Gabrielle felt suddenly icy cold. 'It's something we both need to be aware of, otherwise we're going to find that we have more problems to contend with than merely getting ourselves out of this fix we're in.'

He crawled out of the shelter, leaving Gabrielle staring after him. She wanted to follow him out and tell him in no uncertain terms that he was wrong but he would only have to hold her and kiss her as he had just done to prove it was all lies. She closed her eyes as she summoned up the courage she was going to need to see her through the ensuing days. It was going to be hard enough just to cope with the physical test of surviving in the jungle without this tension between them. It was laughable really: Doyle thought she was an experienced woman with a string of past lovers to her credit! What would he say if she went after him and told him that she was a virgin, that she had never wanted any man before?

The thought was such a temptation that Gabrielle started to scramble from beneath the canopy, then suddenly stopped as she realised exactly what she was doing.

If she told Doyle that, it would be a mistake. He already
affected her more than any man had ever done and to
offer him still more power over her emotions was little
short of dangerous. They had both been thrust into a
situation which was bound to affect their behaviour,
making them say and do, even *feel* things that they might
never have felt before. To allow this desire she felt for
him to be viewed in anything other than that context
would be little short of madness.

CHAPTER FIVE

SWEAT stung her eyes. Gabrielle leant against a thick tree-trunk as she wiped it away with her sleeve, feeling exhaustion dragging at every weary inch of her body. Doyle had set a gruelling pace this morning, hacking away at the jungle with a silent determination which had challenged her to make an objection, but so far she had held her tongue. However, if he didn't let up the punishing pace soon then she would be forced to make some sort of protest. She didn't think she could keep going this way much longer.

She glanced round at where he was cutting through the undergrowth, watching the way he wielded the knife in a slashing arc to break through the wall of trees. Conversation had been kept to a minimum last night and again this morning. They had both been almost comically polite with one another, yet underneath it all that conversation they'd had lay waiting for its chance to emerge again. It wasn't over, that was certain, just temporarily suspended by a kind of tacit consent. But soon all the feelings and emotions which were bubbling below the surface would boil up, and Gabrielle didn't know whether she was looking forward to it or living in dread of that moment.

'Come on. We don't have all day to waste while you stand there daydreaming.'

Doyle's voice was gruff, edged with an irritation which immediately put Gabrielle's back up. She pushed away from the tree, smiling coldly at where he stood, his khaki shirt sticking wetly to his powerful body, his hat pushed back on his head so that she could see the wet, dark strands of hair clinging to his forehead. He hadn't shaved in the few days since they had landed in the jungle and his jaw was dark with beard, giving him an almost dangerous appearance as he stood there glaring at her from those icy eyes.

'Heaven forbid that I should hold you up, Doyle. I mean, is this some sort of new record you're trying to set, cutting a path through umpteen miles of jungle in less time than the first poor fool who tried it?'

He smiled thinly. 'Can't manage the pace, eh, Gabby?'

She tossed her head, sending the damp weight of her hair spilling down her back. 'Oh, I can keep up all right, although I know it must be a disappointment to you to realise it. I was just curious as to why you're going at such a rate of knots, as though a thousand demons are after you? Surely you aren't that eager to get rid of me, are you, Doyle? Not afraid that you might find it difficult to keep to what you said yesterday about not wanting to get entangled with me?' She laughed huskily, lifting her hand to winnow the strands of her hair apart as she watched him from under half-closed lids in a look she *hoped* was seductive. 'My, my, Mr Tough Guy... perhaps you aren't quite so tough after all!'

His face closed, every bone outlined under the tanned skin, but his voice was surprisingly soft when he finally spoke—soft but deadly. 'What's the matter, Gabby? Feeling *hungry*? Or don't you like to think that any man can resist your undoubted charms?' His gaze slid over her from top to toe, coolly insolent as it lingered on each curve. 'Another time and another place and I would be more than willing to oblige, sweetheart, but frankly I'm more interested in getting out of here. So let's cut the *femme fatale* act for now, eh? If you tried employing your energy in another direction then maybe you wouldn't be feeling so tired.'

'It will be a cold day in hell before I'm hungry for you, Doyle! I would rather starve first!' Her voice rose, carrying clearly across the few yards which separated them, but Doyle made no reply as he turned back to his task of hacking through the undergrowth.

Gabrielle glared at his broad back, although in truth she knew it had been her fault for starting it. Why did she seem to feel the urge to goad him at every opportunity, to throw what had happened back in his arrogant face? She had long since learned to control her temper, facing the world and minor irritations with an admirable composure which she knew made her appear rather cold and calculating to many people. Yet it seemed impossible to act that way around Doyle. He seemed to light fires inside her, fires which burned away her veneer of sophistication so that she reacted from instinct.

She slammed her hand against the tree-trunk in a fit of frustration, then gasped when a shower of water and leaves rained down on her head and shoulders. A couple of leaves dropped into the neckline of her shirt and she muttered to herself as she tried to scoop them out again. Her searching fingers brushed against something soft and faintly hairy, and she froze, then let out a shrill scream when whatever it was started to move.

'In the name of God, what is it?' Doyle was beside her, catching her by the shoulders, his fingers bruising as he held her while she struggled frantically to unfasten the shirt and rid herself of the wriggling insect.

'There's something in my shirt... an insect or something. Get it out, Doyle!' There was a note of rising hysteria in her voice and Doyle reacted to it. Catching hold of the front of the shirt, he ripped it open, then plucked the long bright green and yellow caterpillar off her and held it in his hand.

'It's all right, Gabby. It won't hurt you. It isn't poisonous.'

Gabrielle shuddered, averting her eyes from the huge wriggling insect. 'I can't stand anything like that, whether it's poisonous or not.'

Doyle tossed it into the trees, then stared back at her with disgust. 'All this fuss just about an insect. Grow up, Gabby!'

'It isn't my fault if I have a thing about them!' She glared back at him, then realised what a sight she must look with the khaki shirt hanging open, her small, firm breasts barely concealed by the lacy bra. Hurriedly she caught the two edges of the shirt together but it was impossible to fasten it now that all but one of the buttons had been torn off. Taking hold of the two bottom ends, she started to tie them into a knot, then stopped when she suddenly caught sight of Doyle's arm. 'What happened to your arm? It's bleeding.'

'I caught it with the knife when you screamed.' He stared down at the long, thin wound then glanced back at her, his face telling her exactly what he thought of her for doing such a thing as screaming with so little justification. 'Perhaps next time you encounter one of those harmless little insects you could manage to control yourself?'

Gabrielle shuddered. 'It might have been harmless but it was hardly little! Look, Doyle, I am sorry if you cut yourself because of me. Here, let me do something about it.'

She reached out to take hold of his arm, wanting to make amends for the trouble she had caused, but he shrugged her hand off. 'Leave it. I think I can survive without your ministrations. Now, if you're quite sure you can't find any more things to delay us, shall we get on? At this rate our hopes of being picked up are disappearing faster than my patience.'

Doyle drew a handkerchief out of his pocket and wrapped it around the cut, then went back to where he had left the knife and resumed his work without a backward glance in Gabrielle's direction.

Gabrielle poked her tongue out at his back, then flushed as she realised how childish and ridiculous it was. The sooner she and Doyle parted company the better, for both of them!

She glanced down at the gaping front of her shirt and pulled the knot tighter, her hands lingering just for a moment as she looked back at the man who had done nothing but drive her crazy one way or another since they had had the misfortune to meet, and felt a sudden sharp and inexplicable pang at the thought of not having Doyle in her life for much longer. He was infuriating, arrogant, cold and unyielding; he also made her behave totally out of character, as her previous outburst and that ridiculous, childish act of mute defiance proved only too well. But on the other hand he made her feel . . . well, more like a *woman* than she had ever felt in the whole of her life before! It wasn't going to be easy to go back to the person she had been once they parted!

* * *

They came across the small cluster of houses just before
the rain started. They hadn't stopped again, eating the
dry biscuits Doyle had once again produced from the
rucksack while they kept going. Gabrielle had been
praying for the moment when he would announce that
they would stop to shelter from the rain, and breathed
a sigh of relief when he came to an abrupt halt on the
edge of quite a large clearing. However, her relief was
short-lived when she saw the houses.

'Doyle?'

Her voice held a note of uncertainty and he cast her
a level look before glancing back at where people were
starting to appear in front of the huts.

'Just take it easy, Gabby. There are several small
groups of Indians still living in the rainforest and they're
usually quite friendly. I don't imagine that they'll be
looking to add you to the cooking-pot today, if your
luck's in.'

Gabrielle glared at him, hating him for his sarcasm.
'Well, it's odds on that they wouldn't try to make a meal
out of you, mister. You're far too tough and would
probably give them indigestion!'

Surprisingly he laughed at that, his pale eyes filled
with amusement as they scanned her angry face. 'It takes
a lot to put you down, doesn't it, honey?'

He made it sound almost like a compliment. Gabrielle
was so stunned that she just stood and stared at him in
astonishment before hurriedly forcing her attention back
to what was happening as the small crowd of people
started to move towards them.

'Doyle, I don't . . .'

He caught hold of her hand, squeezing it quickly as he pulled her with him to walk towards the group. 'Just keep quiet, Gabby, and leave this to me.'

It was one order she was more than happy to obey, standing silently at his side as he stopped in front of one of the men, who was obviously the leader, and said something to him. Gabby knew that she was staring but it was hard not to do so as Doyle carried out a conversation she couldn't follow, supplementing it with various bits of sign language as he explained how they came to be in the jungle. Where on earth had he learned the language? Obviously he wasn't fluent in it, but he knew enough to make them understand because even as she watched the man started to nod, his lined face breaking into a wide smile. He turned and pointed towards one of the long huts with a thatched roof, obviously gesturing for them to follow him as he led the way across the patch of open ground.

Gabrielle clung on to Doyle's hand, drawing comfort from the feel of his strong fingers clasped around hers as she wove through the group of people. Several of the women reached out to touch her hair and run their fingers down her arm as though they found the sight of her white skin and reddish hair fascinating. Gabrielle did her best not to draw away from their curious hands but was glad when the man led them inside the hut, gesturing for them to sit down on the ground.

It was dark under the thatch and it took a few minutes for her eyes to adjust to the dimness before she could look around. She realised that there were several other people in there, clustered around a child who was lying on some form of bed. Gabrielle watched as a woman, obviously the child's mother, dipped a cloth in water and ran it over his face and down his thin arms, but it seemed to give him little relief because he continued to move restlessly, his small body twisting and turning on the bed.

The man who had led them to the hut said something and one of the women got up and went outside, reappearing just a few minutes later with some food and water which she set out on the floor in front of Doyle and Gabrielle before going back to resume her place by the child. The man smiled at them, gesturing towards the food, obviously urging them to eat, but Gabrielle cast an uncertain glance at Doyle before attempting to help herself to any of it.

'What is it?' she asked softly.

He picked up what appeared to be a piece of flat bread and broke it in two, handing her half. 'Just bread made from manioc, which is cassava, and some fish. It's their staple diet around here. They clear a patch of the rainforest, then burn the trees and spread the ash on the ground. When it rains it washes it into the soil and acts as a fertiliser which enables the Indians to grow their crops.'

'I see.' Gabrielle bit into the piece of bread and chewed it slowly, then took a small piece of the fish, smiling back at the elderly man who was watching them intently. 'It's good.'

Doyle translated what she had said and the man smiled and nodded, urging more food on to them. Gabrielle accepted another small piece of bread, chewing it as she looked curiously at Doyle. 'Where did you learn to speak their language?'

He shrugged dismissively. 'It's always useful to know a few words and it's simple enough to pick it up if you want to. One thing which was always instilled in me when I was doing my training was the importance of being able to converse even on the most basic level.'

'Training? What kind of training? I thought you ran a freight company of sorts?' Gabrielle didn't try to hide her surprise.

'That is part of my job, yes. But it involves all sorts of different things, Gabby,' he said obliquely.

He turned back to the older man, leaving Gabrielle with the distinct feeling that she was missing something. She thought back over all that she knew about Doyle, but it was so little that it told her virtually nothing. Even the letter that her grandfather had sent to her when Doyle had met her had merely stated that she was to accompany the bearer, who would take her to where he was staying. Now she suddenly wished that she had asked more questions, sought more answers, discovered a whole lot more about this man who was starting to play an increasingly important role in her life!

Pondering on the mystery, she let her eyes travel around the dim interior of the hut and found them coming back to rest on the small group of women crouched around the child. Even as she watched, the young woman started to cry silently, her face a picture of total despair which tugged at Gabrielle's heart-strings. Without stopping to think whether it was wise, she got up and went across to them, crouching down beside the child, wishing she could speak their language to ask what was wrong with him.

The women shrank back, leaving only the child's mother to face Gabrielle, who tried her hardest to smile reassuringly at her. Reaching out, she touched the child's cheek with the back of her hand, and was shocked to feel the burning heat of his skin. Obviously he was running a very high temperature, and just as obviously his mother's ministrations were having little effect at controlling it.

When Doyle suddenly appeared beside her, Gabrielle looked up at him with faintly pleading eyes. 'He looks awful, Doyle. Isn't there anything we can do to help?'

He shook his head. 'I doubt it. We have no idea what's wrong with him, and even if we had I'm no doctor—and I don't expect you are either.'

'But there must be something we can do. Can't you ask them if they know what's wrong?' She stared defiantly up at him, her grey eyes daring him to refuse.

'Why should you care what happens to him, Gabby? He isn't your responsibility.'

It was so hard-hearted that she couldn't contain her contempt. 'Perhaps not, but that doesn't mean I'm prepared to sit back when there might be some way I can help!'

For a moment their eyes locked, and Gabrielle felt her heart leap at the expression she saw in Doyle's before it was gone, so fast that she thought she must have imagined it. She looked away, only barely aware of him moving back across the hut and the low hum of voices as he spoke to the old man. Her heart was pounding, her breath so tight that she felt dizzy from trying to suck air into her lungs, and all because for one foolish moment there she had imagined that she had seen something like admiration and a fierce kind of joy blazing in Doyle's eyes. It must have been imagination, of course, because there seemed very little that he found to admire about her!

It took a while before he came back. Obviously his knowledge of the language was limited to essentials and discussing the child's illness through a mixture of sign language and a few words was difficult. However, when he crouched down beside Gabrielle his face was grim enough to make her stomach lurch in sudden apprehension.

'Do you know what's wrong with him?' she asked quietly.

'It's only a guess, but I think he could be suffering from some sort of throat infection. From what I can gather he's been having trouble eating and drinking for a few days now because his throat has been swollen and sore.'

'A sore throat? But he's so ill, Doyle!' She wasn't conscious of laying her hand on his arm until he covered it with his, his tone gentle.

'Illnesses which are just minor to us kill more of these people than anything else. They have no resistance to the common cold, measles, mumps—all those things which we shrug off with the help of the right kind of medicine. The boy had been down at the mission with his mother and he probably picked the germ up there.' He paused, then added quietly, 'They don't think he'll last through the night, Gabby.'

'No!' Her eyes were wide with horror, her face pale as she cast a helpless look at the child. She turned back to Doyle beseechingly. 'We have to do something! Surely you can think of something to do—maybe help take him back to the mission. There must be someone there who would be able to help him.'

He shook his head, staring at the child who was moving restlessly, his small, thin body glistening with sweat. 'He wouldn't survive the journey. It's a good ten days' walk from here.' He got up suddenly, walking back to where he had left the rucksack. Feeling in the side pocket, he pulled out a small bottle of tablets and tossed them in his hand before carrying them back to where Gabrielle was sitting.

'This could do the trick.'

'What is it?' She took the bottle from him, her face lighting up when she read the label. 'Penicillin? Do you think it would work, Doyle?'

'There's a good chance it will if we get him started on it as soon as possible.'

'Then what are we waiting for?' Gabrielle reached up to take the bottle from him, but Doyle's fingers closed around it, his expression very serious now.

'It isn't that straightforward, Gabby. First we have to convince his mother that it could help and then it's a question of administering the dose to the boy. We can't just give him one of these tablets. Apart from the fact that the dosage will be too strong, he won't be able to swallow them. They will need to be crushed and mixed with a drop of water and then be fed to him on a regular basis every three to four hours.'

Gabrielle tossed back her hair as she scrambled to her feet. 'I can't see any problem in that.'

'No?' Doyle arched a brow. He looked big and tough as he stood in the low-roofed hut, his back to the light so that his face was half shadowed, allowing Gabrielle to read little of his feelings. 'It could take a couple of days, Gabby. Two days that we would need to remain here just to make sure that the boy gets the medicine at the right times. It could mean that we miss those search planes. Are you prepared to take that kind of a gamble for a child you don't even know?'

Gabrielle didn't even pause to think, her face betraying how hurt she felt that he should ask such a question. 'I know you will probably find this impossible to believe, Doyle, as I am well aware of the opinion you have of me, but I am prepared to take that chance rather than leave this child to suffer. I'm not quite the selfish, spoilt brat you make me out to be!'

Unexpected tears filled her eyes and she turned away so that he wouldn't see them, but obviously she was just a bit too slow. Doyle stopped her with a gentle hand on her shoulder, tilting her face up to wipe away the moisture with his thumbs in a touch so achingly tender that Gabrielle felt like throwing herself into his arms and bawling, only somehow she managed to control the urge.

'Gabby, I . . .' He seemed strangely hesitant for a man who was always in such control, both of himself and his situation, and she cast him a curious look as she heard him curse roughly. 'I wish to God that I had never agreed to this!'

He let her go and turned away, his back rigid, anger in every powerful line of his body, yet for some strange reason Gabrielle knew that for once it wasn't aimed at her. She stared after him in confusion as she tried to work out what was wrong, but that was like wishing for the moon—something quite beyond her. But somehow, some way she was going to get her answers or her name wasn't Gabrielle Marshall!

She sat down again next to the child, pleased that his mother seemed to accept her presence now, as did the other women who clustered around them. She looked up, her eyes resting on Doyle for a moment while she

felt a strangely inexplicable shiver race down her spine.
When she finally got all those answers, would she then
be sorry?

The night seemed endless. Gabrielle and Doyle main-
tained a vigil at the child's bedside, feeding him the
crushed-up tablets mixed with water. In the early hours
Doyle suggested that she should try to get some sleep
but Gabrielle refused. There was no way that she would
be able to rest with the boy hovering between life and
death.

When the sun came up she left the hut and walked
across the clearing, easing muscles which felt cramped
and stiff from remaining crouched at the child's bedside.
Doyle was still there, waiting to give the boy another
dose of penicillin. Watching the way he had handled the
sick child with such tenderness had shown Gabrielle a
new side to him, far removed from the tough one she
had encountered so far. What an odd mixture he was—
a mystery. On the one hand he could be cold and unyielding and on the other he displayed a compassion
which Gabrielle knew few men possessed, or at least were
willing to display in case others misinterpreted it as
weakness. Doyle apparently had no worries in that respect; he was sure enough of himself not to care what
others felt. He was a rare sort of man indeed.

Tilting her face up to the sun, Gabrielle let her mind
drift over it all, absorbing all the things she had learned
about Doyle in the past few days. He seemed to have
become so important in her life that her thoughts were
rarely free of him. Was it just because fate had thrust
them into such close proximity, or was there some other
reason why her head and heart should be full of him?

The question hovered unanswered before she pushed it aside and turned to walk back to the hut, somehow afraid to let her mind dwell on it too long.

'So there you are. Are you all right?'

Doyle's quiet voice brought her to a halt at the bottom of the steps leading up to the hut. Gabrielle glanced up at him, letting her eyes linger on the weary lines of his face. He looked tired and for some reason it shocked her because tiredness wasn't something she associated with him. He had forged a way for them through the jungle with both strength and determination, and to see him looking suddenly so strangely weary made her heart ache.

'I'm fine,' she replied just as softly as the question had been asked. 'But how about you? You look worn out.'

He came down the steps to stop beside her, running a hand through his dark hair to push it back from his brow before glancing down at her with a faint, dismissive smile. 'Perhaps I'm getting too old for this kind of thing. Spending a whole night awake is taking its toll.'

Gabrielle returned the smile but couldn't quite believe what he had said. Doyle's stamina was far too well-developed for one sleepless night to have made him appear so weary. However, there was little she could say to dispute it so she cast around for something else, oddly reluctant to break this truce which they both seemed to have agreed on without even talking about it. Throughout the long night they had worked side by side, trying to make the child comfortable, and had not exchanged one cross word. That surely must be an achievement to be proud of and not want to spoil!

'How's our patient? Any change?'

Doyle pushed his hands into the pockets of his trousers and hunched his shoulders. 'I think he seems to be just a bit less restless than he was, but I hesitate to say that he's on the mend.'

'When can we expect to know if... if the penicillin has worked?' Gabrielle couldn't bring herself to voice her worst fears, looking away as she felt Doyle look at her. When he laid his hand against her cheek and turned her face back to his she stared back at him with clouded grey eyes which told their own story. He sighed softly, his fingers moving gently against her soft cheek in an almost absent-minded caress which held a trace of familiarity, as though offering comfort in such a way was natural to him. But was it only aimed at her, or would Doyle respond just the same way with any woman in this situation?

'We have done our best, Gabby, and no one can do more than that.' The quiet statement drew her mind away from the oddly hurtful thought and Gabrielle forced a shaky smile, afraid to let him see what she was thinking.

'I know, but sometimes it isn't enough, is it, Doyle? It makes you feel so helpless in a way. I wish there were more I could do, something to ensure that that child recovers!'

He let his hand fall from her and stared across the clearing towards the fence of trees. 'You did more than anyone could have expected you to do last night. You sat there and kept watch over a child who has no claim on your time.'

Her heart ached, the pain so sharp and bitter that Gabrielle stiffened under its force. 'You mean I did more than *you* imagined I would? Isn't that so, Doyle?' She laughed harshly, blinking hard to clear her eyes of the foolish tears. 'You have such a high opinion of me, don't you? Yet if you were really honest you would be forced to admit that you have no basis for it. You know absolutely nothing about me, Doyle!'

'No?' His anger rose so swiftly that Gabrielle took a step back, away from the fury she could see etched starkly on his face and in the glittering, icy depths of his eyes. When he laughed suddenly a shudder ran through her at the contempt she could hear in it. 'I know a lot more about you than you imagine, sweetheart, a whole lot more. But even if I didn't it wouldn't take me long to understand you because I've met people like you before!'

His contempt hurt but it also put a light to her own temper. 'Oh, yes? Tell me more.' She arched a slender brow, staring back at him in an open challenge, but nothing, not even anger, could have prepared her for the shock of what she heard.

'I was married to a woman just like you, Gabby. In fact you're so alike that you could be two peas from the same pod.' His eyes slid from her shocked face and down her still body before returning to meet hers. 'Oh, physically you aren't alike. Elaine was a good-looking woman but you're beautiful, Gabby, as you very well know. But your backgrounds are exactly the same. You both come from families where money is no object, and life is to be lived enjoying one long round of pleasure. So when you accuse me of not understanding what makes you tick, I'm afraid you're way off the mark. I understand you only too well!'

He turned, walked back up the steps and disappeared inside the hut, leaving Gabrielle staring after him with shock. Doyle had been married! Somehow she had never considered that possibility and learning of it now shocked her rigid. She sat down on the bottom step, hugging her arms around her as she stared blankly across the clearing and tried to come to terms with what she'd learned, but it was impossible to do that with this pain tearing her apart.

She could only guess what had gone on in Doyle's marriage. He had spoken of it in the past tense so she must assume that it was over now, but obviously the memory of it was still a bitter one. It explained so much—his attitude towards her, the low opinion he had of her—but it was unfair to judge her because of what some other woman had done!

Admittedly they had got off to a bad start, and if she could take back some of the things she'd said then she would, but surely he could see that she wasn't the selfish, spoilt woman he accused her of being. This trek through the jungle was changing her, making her see things clearly for the first time in years, consolidating all those vague feelings of uncertainty about her life and the direction it was taking. Merely to class her as the same as his ex-wife just because they came from a similar background was both ridiculous and unfair! Yet how did she convince Doyle of that? And why did it seem so important to do so?

She could have her pick of any number of eligible men, men who treated her exactly as she was accustomed to being treated, yet suddenly Gabrielle knew that that meant nothing to her. All she wanted was for one man, one very special man, to accept that he had been wrong in his assessment of her!

CHAPTER SIX

BY THE time night fell there was a marked improvement
in the boy's condition. Gabrielle knelt at his bedside,
watching his mother feed him sips of water. His fever
had broken and his small body was lying quietly now,
the restless movements stilled. The woman looked up at
Gabrielle and smiled, her dark eyes saying everything
the language barrier made it impossible for her to put
into words.

Gabrielle took her hand and squeezed it, letting her
know how pleased she was that the child would recover,
then glanced round when she heard Doyle stopping
beside them. Her eyes met his then skated hurriedly away
as she bent back to the task of crushing another piece
of the penicillin tablet for the boy's next dose. They had
avoided speaking to each other since that exchange on
the steps earlier in the day and Gabrielle had no intention of breaking the silence. In her view it was up to
Doyle to make the first move. How dared he judge her
in terms of another woman?

'He's looking better. Another few hours and I think
he will be well and truly on the mend.'

Gabrielle merely nodded, refusing to answer, and
heard Doyle utter something rough half under his breath.
Reaching down, he took the small wooden bowl from
her and set it aside, then caught her arm to haul her
unceremoniously to her feet. Gabrielle glared at him,
letting him know what she felt of his high-handedness,

although she didn't want to risk disturbing the now
sleeping child by giving full vent to her anger. 'Please
let me go!' she whispered icily, all too aware that the
boy's mother was watching them.

Doyle glanced down at the woman and, with no more
thought, started towards the door of the hut, dragging
Gabrielle after him. Gabrielle's face flamed; she was
aware of the interested glances they were attracting.
Several families shared the communal living-quarters and
it was obvious that they found the sight of her being
frog-marched towards the door of great interest.
However, if Doyle was even aware of the looks they were
collecting he gave no sign, striding down the steps of the
hut and over to the far side of the clearing before he let
Gabrielle go.

'Well, I suppose I'd better hear it.'

'I don't know what you're talking about! Just who
do you think you are, throwing your weight around like
that?' Gabrielle snapped the question at him but didn't
bother to wait for an answer as she turned and started
back the way they had come. She got no further than a
couple of steps, however, before Doyle caught her again,
swinging her round to face him so fast that she almost
overbalanced and would have fallen if he hadn't steadied
her. His hands lingered on her waist for a fraction longer
then was perhaps strictly necessary and Gabrielle felt her
breath catch, her heart shudder to a halt, then just as
abruptly he set her from him. Folding his arms across
his powerful chest, he studied her from under lowered
brows, his eyes silvery in the fading light.

'Let's cut out all the games, shall we, honey? Tell me
what's eating you now.'

'Nothing! There is nothing eating me, nothing wrong that your disappearing off the face of the earth wouldn't cure. *And* I am not your honey. I am not your anything, Doyle! I am especially not a substitute for your wife!'

The words rang around the clearing, echoing back from the trees. Gabrielle bit her lip, wishing she could call them back, but it was too late for that and perhaps it was better that it was out in the open. They would have to spend however many days it took to reach the spot where they would be picked up together, and that was going to be hard enough, without having this resentment she felt building like a huge lump inside her.

Tossing her hair back, she stared defiantly at him, wishing she could tell what he was thinking, but Doyle was a past master at hiding his feelings. 'There is no question of your being a substitute for her, Gabby. Don't be ridiculous.'

'Me? *I'm* the one being ridiculous? Oh, that's rich... really rich!' She took a step towards him, glaring up into his arrogant face with angry grey eyes. 'You tell me that you know what I'm like, *judge* my behaviour and base that judgement on what some other woman has done, and then tell me that *I'm* being ridiculous! Come on, Doyle. Even an arrogant, self-opinionated swine like you must see the error in that!'

His jaw tightened, his big body growing tense at the insults. 'I would watch my tongue if I were you, Gabby.'

'Why? What do you intend to do to me? How will you punish me, Doyle? And will it be me that you're punishing or your wife? I think I can understand why she walked out on you. It must be difficult living with someone like you!'

She spat the words at him, anger taking the edge off
caution, but she wasn't the only one who was furiously
angry, it seemed. His hands closed around her shoulders,
bruising as he hauled her towards him. 'You never learn,
do you, Gabby?'

'What is there to learn? I think I already have a very
good picture of what you're like, Mr Doyle!' She gave
a soft little laugh, feeling excitement curling in the pit
of her stomach as she saw his jaw clench, felt his fingers
biting into her flesh. She was pushing him on along a
route which held a certain amount of danger and it sent
a *frisson* through her as she waited to find out what his
reaction would be.

'You don't know the first thing about me, lady. If you
did, you wouldn't push your luck like this.' He bent to
stare into her face, then suddenly smiled, and the *frisson*
surged into shivers at the expression she saw there. 'Or
am I just a bit slow on the uptake? With your experience
perhaps you *do* know what you're doing and are making
me angry deliberately. Well, I would hate to see all that
effort go to waste, Gabby.'

His head came down, his intention obvious. But because it was suddenly, shockingly, the one thing she
wanted most in the whole world, the one thing which
would explain why she had spoken out like that,
Gabrielle denied herself the pleasure of his kiss, knowing
that to give him so much power when she herself was
so vulnerable would be the biggest mistake she could
make. She pushed him away, her hands fastening around
his forearms as she forced space between them, and heard
Doyle give a low groan of pain which shocked her into
stillness. Hesitantly, she glanced up into his face,
watching the way the colour ebbed from beneath his skin.

'What is it? Doyle?' She shook him, her fingers fastening tighter around his arms as she tried to make him respond, and heard him moan sharply before he bit off the sound. Abruptly he stepped back from her, breaking the hold she had on him, breathing deeply for several seconds as he obviously tried to get control of whatever ailed him.

'Doyle!' Exasperated and worried, Gabrielle stepped forward, but when she moved as though to touch him he drew back.

'Don't!'

Gabrielle studied him in confusion, trying to work out what was wrong. Her eyes fell to where he was cradling his arm in his hand and she frowned as she realised that it was the arm he had cut with the knife the day before. 'Is there something wrong with that cut? Let me see.'

'It's just a bit tender,' he replied curtly.

'Are you sure that's all? Look, Doyle, if there is something wrong with it then tell me. There's no point in trying to play the big tough guy!'

He stared coldly at her, freezing her with the chilling force of his stare. 'There's nothing wrong. Don't let your recent success go to your head, Gabby. Florence Nightingale you are not!'

He walked past her. Gabrielle stared at his retreating figure; she must know every inch of his back by now, because that was what Doyle presented to her most of the time. In a way it seemed to sum up their relationship—if relationship wasn't too strong a word for this armed neutrality they were forced to endure. Doyle was always able to turn his back on her and put her out of his mind while she was doomed to think about him most of the time!

* * *

They left the Indian village at sunrise. The boy was greatly improved, sitting up and drinking water unaided now. There were a lot of thanks, easily understood despite the fact that Gabrielle couldn't follow a word of what was being said. Doyle left the tablets behind, painstakingly miming to supplement his sketchy knowledge of the language until he was sure that the child's mother understood how often and how much of the penicillin to administer.

Gabrielle watched him, marvelling at his patience as he repeated the instructions several times, yet her heart was heavy. Obviously his impatience manifested itself around her but with other people he didn't suffer that same problem. It just served to emphasise how he felt about her.

When she hesitantly suggested that they should head towards the mission he dismissed the idea. It would take ten days' arduous journey to reach it, whereas by his estimation they should be at the point he had given over the radio in less than two. Gabrielle didn't argue with his reasoning, realising that it held a grain of sense. The sooner they were picked up the better, logic told her, but logic didn't have a lot of influence on her emotions. The thought of having just two more days with Doyle before they parted for good was less appealing than it should have been in the circumstances, but she didn't allow herself to dwell on it.

They soon slipped back into the rhythm of fighting a path through the trees but, after an hour or so, Gabrielle knew that there was something different today. They seemed to be moving a lot slower, as though Doyle found cutting through the vegetation more of an effort. There was a jerkiness to his movements which increased as the day wore on. Sweat had soaked into the back of his shirt and when he paused to catch his breath she saw that his skin was grey under the tan, tinged with a thin line of red along each cheekbone which alarmed her.

'Are you feeling all right?' she asked hesitantly, but he merely spared her a quick glance before turning back to the job of hacking through the plants.

'Fine. Now let's get a move on.'

Gabrielle did as he asked, but progress was painfully slow. Doyle stopped to rest more and more often, his chest heaving from the exertion. It was only pigheaded determination which kept him going at all, Gabrielle thought. And if he had any sense he would admit that he felt ill but no, on and on he went, until he was swaying on his feet, his face running with sweat, his pale eyes barely focused.

When Gabrielle stepped forward and took the knife from him he made a token protest, then sank down on to the ground and laid his head back against a tree-trunk, closing his eyes as though it was suddenly too much effort to keep them open any more. Gabrielle dropped down beside him, fear darkening her own eyes to a deep cloudy grey as she reached out and hesitantly touched his shoulder.

'Doyle, you have to tell me what's wrong.'

He seemed to make a supreme effort to look at her then, his mouth twisting into a wry smile which tugged at her heart-strings. 'Stubbornness.' He saw her lack of comprehension and lifted his arm, dragging off the soiled handkerchief which covered the cut, wincing as he did so. 'The cut must be infected. I should have done something about it before, when it first started to give me trouble, but sheer damned stubbornness wouldn't allow me to admit that there was anything wrong.' He met her shocked eyes, then looked away with a weary sigh. 'Serves me right, eh, Gabby? I expect that's what you're thinking, and you'd be justified in doing so.'

Gabrielle glared at him, using anger to control the fear she could feel building inside her. The thin cut of a couple of days ago had been replaced by an angry red swelling which oozed pus. Most of Doyle's forearm looked swollen, and when she gently touched it she could feel heat pulsing under the skin. It was obvious that it needed attending to, and fast, but how? They were heaven knew where in the middle of miles upon miles of jungle without any medical facilities. 'Can you blame me? It was a stupid and reckless thing to do, to ignore such a wound!'

'Afraid you might have to play Florence Nightingale again, honey?' There was faint mockery in his deep voice and in the look he gave her. 'Don't worry. As you have said more than once, I'm tough. I'm sure I shall survive without you being forced to play nurse to me.'

Gabrielle straightened abruptly, hurt that even now he could find the strength to make a dig at her. 'We'll see, I expect, but isn't there a saying about how the mighty fall? You could be glad of my nursing abilities before too long!'

He staggered to his feet, holding on to the trunk of the tree to steady himself, his face hard. 'Don't hold your breath, Gabby. The less you do for me, the better I shall like it. Now let's get going.'

'Going?' She folded her arms across her chest and smiled sweetly into his set face, refusing to let him see how much it hurt her that he should speak to her that way. 'I rather think you're over-ambitious if you expect to get much further in that condition, Doyle. I give you...oh, about another ten minutes, half an hour at the most, and then I imagine that will be it. You will have to call a halt whether you like it or not.'

He picked up the knife, wiping the edge of it down his trouser leg before weighing it in his hand as he looked back at her. 'We shall see.'

He took a reading from the compass, then turned to hack at the greenery, every movement laboured. Gabrielle wanted to beg him to see sense and accept that pushing himself like this was crazy, but she knew any pleas she made would have the opposite effect. Doyle was determined to do things his way, without help or interference from anyone and especially not from her. All she could do was go along with it and wait to see what happened, but it wasn't a comfortable thought realising that she might find herself stranded here with a sick man—a man, moreover, who would prefer to suffer rather than accept any help she offered!

In the end it was almost an hour before Doyle collapsed. Gabrielle had no idea how he had kept going that long, yet when he suddenly crumpled at the knees and fell into a heap in front of her the shock nearly made her follow him down. She sucked in a few steadying breaths, then bent down and managed to roll him over on to his side, her heart bumping painfully when she saw the waxen pallor of his face and the disturbing line of red on each cheek.

'Doyle? Doyle, can you hear me?' She shook him hard, then did it again even harder, but it was impossible to rouse him and fear swamped her. Closing her eyes, she tried to cling on to her control, ordering herself not to panic. The situation was bad enough without her going to pieces as well, but if only she knew what to do!

When Doyle groaned softly her eyes flew open and she bent closer to him, patting his cheek. 'Doyle, can you hear me?'

'I...' He nodded, then swallowed hard, but his voice was still thick and hoarse when he finally managed to speak. 'It's the infection...from the cut. If...if it's not treated soon it could spread.'

Gabrielle bit her lip, fear coiling in the pit of her stomach as she looked down at his swollen arm. She knew so little about such things but enough to understand the dire consequences of that! 'What do you want me to do?'

Doyle tried to sit up and she slid her arm around him, struggling to lever his big frame into a position whereby he could rest back against one of the trees, but he looked so bad, she knew that he could pass out again at any moment. If she was going to help him at all he had to explain to her quickly what must be done. 'Come on, Doyle. Tell me what I have to do!'

The urgency in her voice got through to him because he focused his attention on her, forcing a smile which made her heart ache. He felt rotten but even so he had managed to think about how she felt and try to reassure her. Tears clouded her eyes and she looked down at her hands as she tried to control the urge to cry and cry and never stop.

'I'm not dead yet, Gabby. And I won't be if you try to get a hold of yourself. I know that this sort of thing must be a great inconvenience to one who is used to having everything run smoothly in her life, but that's how it goes sometimes.'

The sharp edge to his husky voice cut like a razor through the fear and she raised her head, colour staining her cheeks as she stared back at him. 'You are a complete bast——'

'Tut, tut! Such language to soil a lady's tongue. I'm shocked at you, Miss Marshall.' His face held a glint of amusement, and Gabrielle didn't know whether to laugh or cry. He had done that deliberately, of course. Made her angry so that she wouldn't lose control. What a scheming wretch he was!

'Not half as shocked as you would be if I really told you what I thought. Now, I suggest you tell me what needs to be done before you pass out again and it's all left to my imagination.' She gave a delicate shudder, glancing at him from under the sooty lashes. 'Finishing-school and debs' parties don't always fit one for this sort of situation, you understand?'

'I don't think they've stood you in too bad a stead, Gabby.'

As a compliment it scored less than one on a count of one to ten, but Gabrielle felt herself glow inside. She was so used to Doyle's putting her down at every opportunity that to hear him now praising her made it all the more valuable. Her face glowed as she stared back at him. 'I shall do my best, Doyle. Just tell me what I need to do.'

He seemed to hesitate for a moment, then spoke quietly. 'The cut needs lancing to allow the poison to escape. You'll have to do it, Gabby. I doubt I'd be able.'

'I...' She bit back the instant refusal, realising that she had little choice. As Doyle had said, there was no way that he would be able to do it himself. 'What...what shall I do first?'

His eyes warmed with approval as he reached out and gave her hand a squeeze. 'Good girl. You can do it, Gabby. I know you can.'

She laughed shakily, curbing the urge to wrap both her hands around his and hang on for dear life. 'Let's hope your sudden confidence in my abilities isn't misplaced, then.'

'It isn't.' He picked up the knife and held it out to her. 'You'll need to wash this as best you can, then I want you to light the stove. You've seen me do it so it shouldn't be too difficult. Then I want you to hold the blade in the flame to ensure that any germs are killed. Then . . .' He shrugged lightly, as though the prospect of what was to come were no more than an inconvenience.

Gabrielle took the knife, holding it gently in her hands for a few long seconds while she tried to find the courage to do as Doyle had asked. She'd never had to do anything like this before and she wasn't sure that she was capable of it. She looked back at Doyle, all her fears hovering on the tip of her tongue, but she let them fade away without giving voice to them as she saw the weary strain on his face, the way he was barely able to move his arm without it causing him pain. If she didn't perform this operation the infection would spread and the consequences of that didn't bear thinking about.

Without a word she got up, calmly carrying out his instructions to the letter, praying that some of Doyle's bravery would rub off on her to carry her through the next few minutes. Frankly, she knew she was going to need it!

Rain was dripping through the rough shelter she had managed to fashion. Gabrielle hunted in the rucksack for the tin mug and positioned it under the drip, then glanced over at Doyle as she must have done a hundred times already. He had passed out while she'd been attending to the wound, slipping silently into a merciful blackness which Gabrielle envied him. It had taken all her courage to do what had to be done but she had managed it somehow. Now all she could do was pray that the infection hadn't had a chance to spread. If it had...

She blanked out that thought, telling herself it was pointless to dwell on something which might never happen. Resting her head back against the rucksack she'd tossed on the ground, she listened to the rather laborious sound of Doyle's breathing. He had come to for a few minutes before, then seemed to fall back to sleep, and she could only hope that it would do him good, help him recover some of that formidable strength he possessed. In just a few short days she had come to rely on him so much, had leant on his strength not only to get them out of this situation but to keep them sane while doing so. If she'd found herself in this situation by herself, or with one of the men from her circle, then she wouldn't have survived so far.

'No! Don't do it...mind out!'

She jumped as Doyle started to shout out loud, his body twisting on the ground beside her. Reaching out, she laid her hand on his shoulder and shook him, but although he quietened he didn't wake. Under her fingers his skin felt burning hot, the shirt soaked with perspiration. Obviously he was running a fever and Gabrielle could have wept. It had been bad enough caring for the Indian child but there had been both her and Doyle then, plus the child's mother and relatives. Now she was all

by herself, and she wasn't sure that she could cope if
Doyle's fever got worse.

She forced the panic down and made herself think
logically about what she had to do, remembering only
too clearly how the boy's mother had sat by his side,
sponging him down. She would try that, would sponge
Doyle down and pray that his temperature would drop,
because there was nothing else to help control it. He had
left all the penicillin tablets behind in the village.

The time dragged past. Gabrielle's arms and shoulders
were aching with wiping the cloth over Doyle's face and
down his throat. By the time night fell she was functioning automatically, her hands smoothing up and
down, back and forth, as though they had been pro-
grammed to repeat the ceaseless motion. Doyle kept half
rousing from the heavy sleep he was in, only to sink
back again just as her hopes were rising that this was
the breakthrough she was praying for. Then suddenly
he started to mutter again, his body shaking.

Gabrielle dropped the cloth and bent closer to him.
'Doyle! Can you hear me?'

'Cold. So very cold, Gabby.' As though to emphasize
what he was saying he hugged his arms around himself,
his body racked with spasms. Gabrielle felt tears of
helplessness prick her eyes; cooling him down didn't seem
half so difficult as trying to keep him warm without the
aid of blankets or anything else to cover him with. What
should she do?

She took hold of his hand between both of hers and
rubbed it, trying to put some warmth back into his fever-
chilled body, but after several minutes realised it was
wasted effort. Doyle was still shaking, his teeth chat-
tering with cold despite the fact that the air temperature

must have been in the eighties. Rubbing his hands would have little if any effect against the cold he was feeling. She needed to warm his body up all over, not just part of it.

Taking a deep breath, Gabrielle lay down on the ground next to him and gathered him into her arms, holding him close so that the warmth from her body flowed into his, but even then it took a long time before it seemed to have much effect. Sliding her arms more firmly around his lean waist, she inched herself closer, feeling his breath stirring the hair at her temples. It was an oddly disturbing feeling to be this close to him, to feel every hard inch of his powerful body imprinted on her own, to feel his chest pushing against her breasts with every breath he took. Doyle was hard and tough and to see him now at his most vulnerable evoked feelings inside her she had never expected to feel for any man!

With a low sigh Gabrielle snuggled closer, resting her head in the hollow between his neck and shoulder while she closed her eyes the better to savour the sensations holding Doyle like this aroused. What would it feel like to have the right to do this all the time, to hold Doyle and be held by him? As she drifted off to sleep, Gabrielle realised that that would be a rare kind of gift indeed.

There was a bird singing high above them. The sound carried through the still morning air, pure and sweet, bringing Gabrielle awake with a smile on her lips.

'Mmm, I wonder if that smile is for me?'

Doyle's low voice seemed in harmony with the morning peace and Gabrielle smiled again, arching sleepily. She felt more relaxed than she'd felt for years, her whole body warm and contented. When she felt a hand smooth her cheek she turned her face towards it, nuzzling into the palm, and heard Doyle laugh very softly, very gently, but in a way which made her heart leap.

'I could get used to waking up with you beside me, Gabby. Very used to it indeed.'

So could she. She could easily slip into the habit of waking, feeling warm and cared for, to find Doyle beside her, his hard body touching hers while he ran his hand over her in those disturbingly soft caresses. Her eyes opened, the smile lingering on her full lips as she studied the angular lines of the face so close to hers for a long moment before suddenly reality returned with a swiftness which drove every foolish thought from her head. 'Doyle, I...!'

'Don't spoil it, Gabby.' His eyes were suddenly fierce as they claimed hers, his hand holding her head as she tried to turn away from a look which seemed to cut right through to her soul. Tension seemed to arc between them, so raw and powerful that it scorched the air, cast a spell which neither of them seemed able to break. Then, slowly, so slowly that it had a dream-like quality, Doyle lowered his head and took her mouth in a long, drugging kiss, and all thoughts of moving fled abruptly from Gabrielle's mind.

When he drew her closer to him to run his hand down the slender curves of her body Gabrielle shuddered at the tide of sweet sensation it left behind. Every inch of her felt alive, her nerves throbbing with sensation, her blood surging along her veins. She murmured softly, helplessly, her lips clinging to his to return the kiss, and felt Doyle shudder too, felt the betraying surge his body gave as he pulled her against him. When his hand slid to her breast to brush the sensitive peak with his thumb she gave a tiny moan, turning her head so that she could press kisses along the line of his jaw. Her reaction seemed almost to shock him because his hands stilled, then, as though driven by a force beyond his control, it moved to her other breast, repeating the erotic caress with just as devastating an effect.

'Gabrielle, I . . . Oh, hell! Who needs words, sweet, at a time like this?' There was a ragged note in his deep voice which hinted at his own feelings and Gabrielle gloried in the fact that for once he wasn't completely in control. Deliberately she arched against him, letting her breasts brush against his chest, loving the way ripples ran through each muscle in his body. When he started to draw back from her she gave a tiny murmur at the unwanted rejection, then felt her pulse leap when he bent and roughly brushed her parted lips with his, his eyes like pale fire as they burned into hers. 'I want to see you, Gabby, want to touch you without the restriction of clothing. I want to convince myself that I didn't dream how beautiful you looked that day at the pool.'

There was such an aching need in his voice that Gabrielle made no move to stop him as he untied the knot at the front of her blouse and drew the edges apart to stare down at her small, firm breasts, barely concealed by the lacy bra. When his gaze lifted back to her face there was strain etched in it, showing her clearly the control he was exercising over his emotions.

'You're beautiful, Gabrielle,' he said quietly. 'I want very much to make love to you, but it will be your decision.'

'I . . .' Colour ebbed and flowed in her face, her emotions in a storm. She wanted Doyle. There was no point in denying it, no reason to lie. But was wanting something enough? Would making love with him now be a memory to treasure through all the long years to come, or would it be something to regret?

He must have seen her uncertainty because his face closed up. Carefully, almost impersonally, he drew the edges of her shirt together and refastened them, then stood up.

'Doyle, I...' She couldn't think what to say, how to explain that what he had suggested had meant too much to her to be treated lightly.

'Don't worry about it, Gabby. It was just one of those things. I woke up to find you all wrapped around me and nature took its natural course.'

She wanted to cry at his cool assessment of the situation, but pride forbade that she do that. 'I understand. No hard feelings, then?'

'None at all.' He glanced down at his arm, flexing it carefully. 'You did a good job yesterday, honey. A very good job. Ten out of ten, in fact.'

She didn't want his praise or his marks! She wanted...wanted... She didn't know what she wanted, if the truth be told! 'Thank you.' Her voice was calm, giving no hint of what she was really feeling, all those turbulent emotions swirling around inside her. 'I was worried last night. You were running a bit of a fever then all of a sudden you started muttering that you were cold.' She shrugged as she sat up and pushed her fingers through her hair to ease the snarls out of it. 'That's why I resorted to communal body heat, and it seemed to do the trick.'

'It did indeed. Now I think I'll get the stove lit and make us something to eat. I don't know about you but I'm starving.'

He left the shelter and Gabrielle could hear him moving around outside but she made no attempt to go and help him. Doyle had undoubtedly been correct in stating that waking up to find her lying so intimately against him had made nature take its course. He was a normal, healthy male and his body would respond to finding a woman close and seemingly willing. But was that explanation enough to excuse her own responses? Had being in the jungle stripped her emotions to basics? She'd never experienced desire until she'd met Doyle, never wanted to make love with a man. But she had wanted to do so with Doyle, and there didn't seem any easy way to explain that!

CHAPTER SEVEN

THEY made good progress that day. It was a mark of Doyle's strength that he should be able to shrug off the illness of the previous day. Gabrielle insisted on checking the wound at regular intervals but there was no doubt that it was healing now that the infection had been removed. She bandaged it with a piece cut from the tail of her over-large shirt but, despite the strenuous effort involved in hacking through the trees, the dressing remained clean of any blood.

The day followed the pattern of all the others; Gabrielle knew the routine so well by now that it felt as if she'd been living this way all her life. What was it going to be like when they finally left the jungle and returned to civilisation? She thought about it as she followed on Doyle's heels, recalling how she had used to fill her days, yet it felt as though she was watching a film. The endless pursuit of pleasure, the lunches and shopping and skiing, seemed so very distant from this existence. With a jolt she realised that she wasn't looking forward to resuming her previous life. Being in the jungle, forced to fend for herself, seeing that child fight to survive, even dealing with Doyle's illness had changed her irrevocably, and she could never go back to what she had been. She owed it to herself to do more with her life than waste it.

They came across the abandoned remains of an Indian village just as the rain started. Doyle had seemed intent on making as much progress as possible to make up for what they had lost the day before and Gabrielle had been too engrossed in her own thoughts to query his decision not to stop to build a shelter.

Now as the first few spots fell from the sky she ran with him across what must have been the area where the Indians had grown their crops and up the steps into one of the huts. Part of the roof had fallen in and the whole place smelled strongly of damp and decay, but at least it offered some protection from the downpour. Without the protective canopy of leaves overhead the rain fell straight down, pouring from the sky to churn up the earth and run in rivers towards the treeline.

Gabrielle eased the rucksack off her back then went to stand at the door while she watched the ground turn into a muddy swamp. When Doyle came to stand next to her she spared him a glance then turned back to her study of the scene, all too conscious of the fact that her pulse was beating a shade or two faster than usual, thanks to his nearness.

'Why do the Indians abandon their houses like this?' She swept a hand towards the open ground where even now the jungle was starting to break through, claiming back the land. 'I mean, it must take an awful lot of hard work to clear enough ground to grow food yet they just up and leave it. It doesn't make sense.'

Doyle leant a shoulder against the edge of the doorway, following her gaze. 'They have to move around. The land is highly fertile if the forest is left undisturbed but it's a delicate balance. Leaves and dead wood drop to the ground and decompose in time to provide nutrients for other plants but once areas are cleared that chain is broken. The Indians understand that. As I told you, they clear a small patch of forest, burn the trees and use the ash to fertilise the ground, but within a couple of years at most of growing crops the ground's fertility is exhausted. They then have to move on and repeat the whole process.'

'It sounds an awfully hard life. Why do they still do it? Surely it would be possible for them to move into other areas where it wouldn't be so hard just to exist?'

Doyle glanced at her, his face betraying little. 'Perhaps this is the life they prefer to lead, the one they know and understand, rather than face change. Brazil is a country full of natural riches but many poor people, and land is at a premium. This may seem like a dreadful existence to you, Gabby, compared to how you live, but the Indians manage and take a certain pride in doing so.'

'Why do you always try to make me feel guilty?' Anger sparkled in her eyes, added a touch of colour to her skin. 'It isn't my fault that I was born rich, Doyle, the same way as it isn't the fault of anyone who is born poor!'

'Perhaps not, but it's how you live your life and what you do with it that turns it into a crime. You squander your talents, and that's something you should feel guilty about.'

He had only said what she'd been thinking all day, but it struck home too sharply for Gabrielle to admit it to him. 'And you, no doubt, lead a completely blameless and noble existence. Is that what you want me to believe?'

'I don't care what you believe if you want the truth, honey. By tomorrow all this will just be a fading memory. You and I will go our separate ways and that will be that.'

'And you won't ever give me a second thought after that. Am I right?' She laughed harshly, not trying to conceal how bitter she felt. 'It's a good job that I had the sense not to take you up on your offer this morning, then, isn't it? One-night—or should I say one-morning?—stands are not my scene!'

'Then what is your scene?' Doyle's eyes swept over her rigid figure, a strange expression in their depths. 'Come on, Gabby, why pretend to be something you aren't?'

'I am not pretending! You may think you know all about me but you have no real idea at all of how I feel!' She was shaking so hard that she could hardly speak, pain and anger stirring her emotions to boiling-point. 'Your view of me is coloured by what happened in your own marriage. You don't see me, Gabrielle Marshall, as a person in her own right who deserves to be judged on her own merits, but as some shadow of your wife!'

'My marriage has nothing whatsoever to do with you!' He turned to walk away, anger evident in every inch of his body, but if he thought he could turn his back on her yet again he was mistaken.

Gabrielle stepped in front of him, tilting her head to stare straight into his eyes. 'What happened, Doyle? Did your poor wife finally realise she couldn't live with such a self-righteous paragon any longer? Did she walk out on you? Did it injure that massive ego of yours?'

A pulse beat heavily in his jaw, but his tone remained level. 'What happened is none of your concern.'

'Oh, but I disagree. If I'm to be judged according to another woman's actions then I think it's very much my concern!'

'Why should you care what I think of you?'

'I...' She bit her lip, unable to find an easy answer to that seemingly simple question.

'It's highly unlikely that our paths will cross once we're rescued, so what difference does it make that I don't hold a high opinion of you?'

Doyle's voice had dropped, yet it seemed to hold a note which made every nerve in Gabrielle's body tingle with awareness. Under that question there seemed to be another, far more disturbing, far more important. She licked her suddenly parched lips, then felt her breath catch when she saw how Doyle's eyes followed the movement of her tongue. When he took a slow step towards her she backed away, suddenly uneasy, then stopped when she came up against the rough wooden wall of the hut.

'This is starting to get silly, Doyle. I really don't——'

He cut her off as though she hadn't spoken, his pale eyes blazing with light as they stared deep into hers. Gabrielle had the feeling that he was searching for something—but what? What did he want from her? And what did she really want from him? 'It hurts that I should think badly of you, doesn't it, Gabby? I have seen it in your face even though you've done your best to hide it from me. But what would you say if I told you that I might be changing my mind? That I might realise there is more to you than I'd been led to believe?'

There was something odd about what he had said but she couldn't quite put her finger on it, not with her thoughts in such turmoil. 'I thought I was everything you dislike!'

'Perhaps what has happened in the past few days has changed my opinion. I never imagined that the woman

I met at the airport would sit all night with a sick child that she didn't know, nor that she could cope with dressing that cut on my arm and nursing me.'

Neither could she have imagined herself doing such things! But, as she'd admitted to herself before, she had changed in these past arduous days; in a way she had grown up, but would Doyle believe her if she tried to tell him that? Suddenly she was afraid—afraid of telling him that she had learned so much that she would never go back to the life she had led, that she intended to use her talents, not waste them, in case he mocked her as he had done so many times before. And, because it was so important to her, Gabrielle made light of it. 'Anyone would have done the same. It has hardly fitted me for sainthood. After all, if you hadn't recovered I would have been in a real fix!'

He withdrew from her, his face settling into the cynical lines she had grown to recognise. 'I should have realised that your number one concern is always you. I imagine that recounting the touching tale of how you sat by a sick child's bedside will give you something to dine out on for years. There can't be many of your friends who can better that.'

Sickness welled into Gabrielle's stomach but she forced it down, refusing to let him see how once again he had hurt her. It was her fault for not telling him the truth, but maybe it was better to leave it unsaid rather than make herself any more vulnerable. 'How well you seem to know me,' she said quietly.

'Too well to be taken in by any act you put on, Gabby.'

He moved away and sat down on the floor, tipping his hat over his eyes. Gabrielle let her gaze rest on him for a moment more, then turned back to stare out of

the door, watching the rain beating into the ground, and
the dismal greyness of the scene seemed to mirror exactly
the greyness in her heart.

The jungle was closing in on her, the trees reaching out
to catch at her clothes as she struggled to break through
the green wall which imprisoned her. Gabrielle tore at
the clutching branches, trying to rip them off her clothes,
her arms, her legs, but each time she freed one bit the
plants wrapped themselves around another, holding her.

She whimpered softly, twisting and turning, fighting
to get free, but it was impossible to break the hold the
plants had on her. They were drawing her deeper and
deeper into their midst, the trailing greenery winding
around her body, layer upon layer, holding her so tightly
that it was becoming difficult to breathe. With her final
breath Gabrielle screamed . . .

'Wake up! Come on, Gabby. You're dreaming. Wake
up!' Hands shook her roughly, but it was hard to rouse
herself from the terror of the nightmare. It filled her
mind, clinging like the plants, and she gave another shrill
cry of fear which stopped abruptly when a hand caught
her a stinging blow across the cheek, bringing her back
to reality with a jolt.

'You . . . you hit me!'

Doyle's hands relaxed their punishing grip on her
shoulders, but he didn't remove them completely. 'I had
to. You wouldn't wake up.'

Gabrielle shuddered, closing her eyes for a moment
before opening them to look into his face. He had
switched on the torch and set it on the ground beside
them so that its beam enclosed them both in a pool of
golden light beyond which the jungle lay blackly. 'It was

horrible,' she said shakily. 'The plants had a hold of me and each...each time I tried to get free they dragged me back and held me tighter!'

He rubbed his hands up and down her arms in a gesture of comfort. 'It was just a bad dream, Gabby. Try not to think about it. We both need to get some sleep. It's the last leg of the journey tomorrow.'

He started to move away but Gabrielle clutched hold of his arm, her fingers digging into the hard muscles. 'How can you be sure? What happens if the search has been called off? Then what are we going to do, Doyle? Tell me!' There was a note of rising hysteria in her voice and she bit her lip to contain it, hating to let Doyle see her go to pieces this way. It was just that dream, that horrible feeling of being helpless, which still lingered.

'We'll be fine, honey. Trust me. Your grandfather won't have abandoned you so soon.'

'But what if the search has moved further afield or nobody even picked up that radio message you sent before we came down? We could be stuck here forever!'

'Now you're just starting to get hysterical. Stop it, Gabby. It won't help.' His voice was curt, telling her all too plainly what he thought of her fears, yet she couldn't be comforted by his reassurances.

'Silly me. Fancy getting hysterical at the thought of being lost in this damned jungle for years!' She sat up and glared at him, using anger to conquer her rising fear. 'Admit it; you can't be one hundred per cent certain that we will be picked up tomorrow, or the day after, or the year after, can you?'

He seemed to hesitate, a strange expression on his face—unless it was the glow cast by the torch highlighting the angular planes and hollows. 'I cannot see any point in worrying about something which may never happen. Now, let's get some sleep.'

He drew away from her restraining hold, lying down on the ground a few yards away from her before switching off the torch to plunge them into blackness once more. Gabrielle lay quite still, forcing herself to grow accustomed to the total darkness again, but it was hard to shake off the memory of the nightmare and the ensuing sense of dread that they were doomed to remain here in the jungle. A small sob welled from her throat and she pressed her hand against her mouth to hold back all the others which threatened to follow it. She wouldn't cry. She wouldn't start to act like a baby and allow Doyle to laugh at her as he was bound to do.

Curling herself into a tight little ball, she strove to keep control of herself, but it was hard to do that now that the nightmare had stripped away all her resilience. The sob curled from her lips, sounding unnaturally loud in the silence, and she heard Doyle utter a low curse.

'For heaven's sake, what's the matter now?'

His abruptness made her want to cry all the harder and she had to choke back the sobs, then felt every nerve in her body jump when strong hands caught her and rolled her into the solidness of a hard male body.

'Come on, Gabby. It will be all right. You'll see.'

His voice was soft and gentle, far gentler than she'd heard it for ages, and it just made the tears flow faster.

'Don't Gabby. It won't help.' He ran his hand over her hair, smoothing it away from her wet cheek. 'You'll make yourself ill, crying like this.'

'What does it matter? You wouldn't care one way or the other.' Her voice was choked with tears, misery in every flat syllable, and she felt Doyle's hand still against her cheek.

'I care, Gabby. I care far more than I should and that's the damned trouble!'

There was a harsh note of self-condemnation in his deep voice which brought her head up. Gabrielle stared through the darkness, trying to see his face, but the night was just too black for her to see anything. All she could rely on was instinct, and for once she allowed it to be her guide.

She laid her hand against his warm chest, feeling the steady beating of his heart against her palm. 'You have a funny way of showing that you care,' she said softly.

His hand captured hers, pressing it harder against his chest, holding it there while his heartbeat pounded from him into her. 'Maybe it was the only way I could handle what was happening between us, Gabby.'

Her own heart gave a tiny lift of joy. 'And what exactly has been happening, Doyle?'

He laughed huskily, his hand lifting to stroke her cheek and down the smooth column of her throat before stopping so that his fingers lay gently on the pulse at its base. 'I don't really need to answer that, do I, Gabrielle? You feel it too, don't you? That's one of the reasons why we've fought so many times.'

She couldn't deny what he said. There had been an attraction between them from the outset, yet both had fought against it and fought each other in doing so. But suddenly, in the dark silence of the night, Gabrielle no longer wanted to fight. 'I'm not fighting now, Doyle.'

His whole body went rigid; Gabrielle had the feeling that he was fighting some silent inner battle, but then she felt the tension ease out of him, felt the soft brush of his mouth against her hair, the gentleness of his hands as they skimmed the soft curves of her body to draw her closer to him, and all thought fled in the face of sensation. Every soft stroke of his hands against her flesh made her shudder, each touch of his lips sent heat shimmering along each nerve until she was whimpering helplessly, wanting the release only he could give her from the sweet torment.

He drew away from her, reaching for the torch and switching it on so that the soft golden light formed a pool with them as its centre. Then, holding Gabrielle's gaze, he unfastened her shirt and drew it down her arms, tossing it aside before turning his attention to the twine knotted at the waist of her trousers. Gabrielle lay still, watching the shifting play of emotions which crossed his strong face, the naked, mounting desire he made no attempt to hide. Then, when he had finished stripping her, his eyes silver flames as they traced each beautiful curve of her body, she sat up slowly and slid her hands up his chest to undo the buttons of his shirt, pushing it open to press tiny, fleeting kisses to the hard, tanned muscles.

'Gabby, I... Oh, hell, honey, this might be madness but what sweet madness!'

He pushed her back on to the ground, taking his weight on his forearms as he kissed her hungrily. Gabrielle responded just as hungrily, wanting to let him know that she desired him just as much as he desired her. Their mouths met, clung, then drew away, only to return again and again as though neither could get enough of the drugging kisses which fired their blood. When Doyle drew back to cover her breast with his mouth she arched towards him, a small moan escaping from her lips, her hands fastening behind his head to hold him to her. She had never tasted this heady, sensual joy before; had never wanted to. It was only with Doyle that she felt this hunger in her blood, only with Doyle that she wanted to share this moment of intimacy. Only Doyle whom she loved.

The realisation slipped into her mind softly, without bells ringing or horns blowing. It needed no fanfare to announce itself; it just came and made sense out of so much which had made little sense before. She loved Doyle. Why or how didn't matter. It was true.

There was love in her eyes as she framed his face between her hands and pressed her mouth to his in a kiss which made a shudder shake his body. There was love in the way she opened her arms and drew him to her so that their flesh met and merged. And love even in the half-stifled gasp of pain when her untutored body allowed him entry. He went still, shock glittering in the depths of his silver eyes.

'Gabby!'

Gabrielle smiled up at him, her face alight with all she felt. 'See, Doyle, you didn't know *everything* about me!'

Then there was no room for words, no room for anything but the driving need to reach fulfilment, a need which took them to the stars... and beyond.

It was the second time in as many mornings that Gabrielle had woken in Doyle's arms. It was starting to become a habit, and one she had no intention of trying to break!

Easing over, she let her eyes linger on the strong lines of his face, studying each line with a fresh appreciation. Why had she never noticed before just how long his dark brown lashes were, or how perfectly shaped his ears? Each new discovery was a secret joy to be stored and savoured, something fresh to enjoy about this man she had fallen in love with. She wanted to jump right up and shout it aloud, let the world share her discovery, but perhaps it would be better to wait until Doyle was awake and tell him first!

A smile curled her mouth at the thought of what it would be like to tell him, and she closed her eyes and rested her head back on its warm, hard, muscular cushion as she tried to decide what she should say. Somehow waiting until he awoke and coming out with the statement 'I love you' seemed a trifle blunt. The first uncertainty slid coldly through her joy and she frowned. What if Doyle didn't believe her or, worse still, didn't want her to love him? Then what would she do?

Her eyes opened abruptly to rid herself of the unwelcome scenario and she felt her heart bump hard when she saw that Doyle's eyes were open and that he was watching her. For a moment Gabrielle felt as though she couldn't breathe, frozen by the remoteness in that silver-blue gaze, then he spoke and the moment fled.

'You should have told me, Gabby.'

Colour flowed into her face and she looked away, but Doyle turned her head back, brushing her mouth with a far too brief kiss. 'We can't change what happened but perhaps we can make sense of it. And the first thing we must talk about is why you let me make love to you when it was obvious you had allowed no other man that right.'

He was giving her the opportunity she had wanted before, a chance to explain how she felt about him, but suddenly Gabrielle was afraid. 'It was something we both wanted.'

'Yes. I don't deny that, although I wish to God that I had been strong enough to resist!'

'You mean that you...you're sorry that it happened?' It was impossible to hide the pain she felt and she heard Doyle curse before he bent and kissed her with devastating thoroughness.

'I am sorry that it happened last night, but I'm not sorry that it happened.'

He must have been speaking in riddles, because it made no sense at all to her. But as he bent and kissed her again, this time taking his time to draw a response from her, Gabrielle suddenly didn't care. Their passion had been lying dormant and now it erupted so that they made love with a hunger which verged on desperation.

When at last they lay side by side, hands linked, bodies touching gently from breast to thigh, Gabrielle sighed softly. Lifting Doyle's hand to her mouth, she pressed a kiss to his palm then held it against her cheek. 'What's going to happen when we get back, Doyle?' Her voice held a note of uncertainty, and she felt him turn to look at her but made no attempt to meet his gaze.

'You mean when we're picked up?'

Gabrielle nodded, wondering why she felt suddenly chilled. 'Yes. What will happen...with you and me?'

The question seemed to hang in the air for so long that she thought he wasn't going to reply to it. But then he spoke, his deep voice flat and totally unemotional. 'I suggest we wait to see what happens, Gabby. There are...a lot of things which need to be discussed.'

What was there to talk about apart from the fact that she loved him? Gabrielle rolled on to her side, her mouth opening to tell him that, but he stopped her with a gentle finger pressed against her lips. 'Leave it, honey. Let's not make any rash promises just yet.'

He rolled to his feet and started to drag his clothes on, and after a few long minutes Gabrielle did the same thing. From where she stood there was nothing rash about it, but if that was the way that Doyle wanted to play things then she would go along with it... for now! But one thing was certain, and that was that she wasn't going to wait forever!

After what had happened Gabrielle half expected Doyle's attitude to change towards her in some slight way but it didn't. He was just as brusque when he issued his instructions as they carried on with their journey. Yet several times Gabrielle looked up to find him watching her, a strange expression on his face which somehow managed to make her heart beat faster and fill her with a sense of foreboding which she tried to dismiss as purely fanciful. There was nothing to be scared about; Doyle might be as surprised as she by what had happened between them but somehow they would work it out. He had said nothing about his feelings but if actions were anything to go by then he had to *care* about her. He couldn't have made love to her the way he had last night and then again this morning if he felt nothing.

Gabrielle was so lost in her thoughts that she started to lag behind a bit. Realising it, she quickened her pace, wiping the perspiration out of her eyes as she hurried to catch up with Doyle, but when she reached him he had already stopped. He turned to look at her, his silver-blue eyes shimmering in the greenish light. Gabrielle looked at him curiously, then gasped when he suddenly bent and kissed her hard on the mouth. He drew back almost at once, turning to hack away a huge piece of fern with an almost vicious downward swipe of the knife.

Gabrielle pressed her hand to her burning lips, unable to explain why she suddenly felt afraid. She stumbled after Doyle, then came to a shocked halt when she found herself on the edge of a large clearing. For a moment she stared uncomprehendingly at the plane standing at the far side, then turned to Doyle with wide, questioning eyes.

'Is . . . is that your plane?'

'Yes.'

'But I don't understand! Why have we come back here?' Fear was clutching hold of her heart, turning her whole body to ice. 'Doyle!'

He looked at her then, his face betraying nothing. 'Your grandfather hired me to take you into the jungle.'

'What?' She shook her head, all the colour draining from her face. 'No, I don't believe you! You're saying that this has all been some sort of . . . of trick? That we didn't have to land because there was nothing wrong with the plane?'

'That's correct. The engine is working perfectly.'

'But how . . . ? I mean, why? Why on earth did Grandfather do such a thing?' It was hard to believe what she was hearing, hard to understand. This whole journey had been some sort of elaborate plan!

'He had his reasons, but I'm sure that he would prefer to tell you what they were.' Doyle glanced at his watch, his expression never altering. He looked as cool and remote as ever and suddenly Gabrielle felt a pain so sharp that it felt as though her heart was being ripped apart. Grandfather might have instigated this crazy plan for

whatever reason, but Doyle had gone along with it from
start to finish!

'And what about your reasons, Doyle? Why did you
agree to it?' Her voice was so low that for a moment
she thought he hadn't heard her, but then he spoke, no
emotion in his deep voice.

'I was hired to do the job, Gabby.'

'Hired?' She laughed out loud, hearing it echo round
and round the trees, as though a thousand voices were
repeating her laughter, and so they might. Most people
would laugh at what a fool she had made of herself!
'My grandfather paid you to arrange all this? But how
far did he expect this *charade* to go? Was sleeping with
me part of the job, Doyle, or just a small bonus on top
of the agreed payment?'

His face tightened, his eyes burning. For a moment
Gabrielle thought he was going to speak, and steeled
herself for whatever he said, for each word which would
add to the agony inside her. Then without a word he
walked past her towards the plane.

'Damn you, Doyle! I shall never forgive you for this!'

Her voice broke on a sob, but if he heard it he gave
no sign—or was it more that he didn't care? The
job was over; his part had been played. Why should he
care that Gabrielle was left with a broken heart and
shattered dreams?

CHAPTER EIGHT

THE sound of voices carried from the room below into her bedroom. Gabrielle lay on the bed, listening to the rise and fall of them without hearing a word of what was being said. Her grandfather was in his study talking to Doyle, and although she hated herself for her weakness she found herself straining to identify Doyle's deep tones in the conversation.

Rolling on to her side, she tried to blank out the sound, but that was impossible. Her body seemed to be attuned to Doyle's presence, honing in on the familiar hum of his deep voice. What were he and Grandfather talking about? How successful their plan had been?

Pain tore into her heart and Gabrielle swung her legs off the bed and walked slowly over to the window to stare out across the smooth green fields. Her grandfather had been waiting when the helicopter had landed in front of the sprawling ranch-house. He had taken her into his arms and hugged her hard before setting her from him and studying her with concern. Gabrielle had spent the whole flight going over it all in her head, desperately trying to understand why the old man should do such a crazy thing. Yet oddly, when the moment had arrived to ask her questions, she'd no longer felt any desire to hear the answers. It didn't seem to matter any longer; Henry Marshall must have had his reasons— better ones, she didn't doubt, than Doyle had had for agreeing to take part in the plan. Doyle's main reason had been money. He had been hired to take her into the jungle and make sure that no real harm befell her. She only hoped that he thought every tainted penny was worth it!

There was a light knock at the bedroom door and Gabrielle swung round, colour swimming into her pale cheeks, but it was only the young housemaid, bringing a message to ask her to join her grandfather in the study if she felt up to it.

Gabrielle waited until the young girl had left then walked slowly to the huge walk-in wardrobe set along one side of the beautiful, airy room. She had already discovered that her bags had been brought to the house and her clothes hung neatly on hangers ready for her.

Idly she ran her fingers over the expensive garments, letting silk and satin and cashmere slide across her fingertips, and felt tears sting her eyelids as she realised that she would willingly swap all of these for creased khaki. But all that was over now, those days in the jungle were past and she had to get on with the rest of her life. Nothing had ever seemed so daunting.

Slipping an elegant dark blue silk dress from its padded hanger, she laid it on the bed, then added underwear and shoes, even a pair of gold tear-drop earrings. She had no idea if Doyle would be downstairs but if he was then she was going to look her best, arm herself with an outer show of composure and normality. Inside her heart might be breaking, but there was no way that she would ever let him know that. She had been a fool once but she wouldn't be one again!

Fifteen minutes later Gabrielle stood outside the door to the study, feeling her heart pounding. It was one thing to tell herself that she would never let Doyle know how she was feeling and quite another to achieve it when every nerve in her body was stretched to breaking-point at the thought of the coming meeting. However, when she entered the room she found only her grandfather there, standing by the window.

He turned to look at her, smiling as he studied the picture of elegance she made in the slim blue dress. 'Well, it doesn't appear to have done you any harm, darling, living rough for a few days.'

Gabrielle made no reply. What had happened had left scars on her so deep that she doubted they would ever heal, but pride dictated that she tell no one that, not even her grandfather whom she loved dearly. Walking across the room, she joined the old man at the window, her gaze taking in the same view that she had seen from her bedroom window. 'Why did you do it, Grandpa?'

Henry Marshall sighed softly. 'Because I was worried about you, Gabrielle.'

'Worried?' She turned to stare at him, not trying to hide her disbelief and hurt. 'You arranged to have me...me stranded in the middle of the jungle because you were *worried* about me?'

He took her hand and led her over to the huge leather sofa, patting the seat beside him as she remained standing. 'I know you must be angry, darling. All I ask is that you allow me to explain. Then perhaps you will understand that although it must seem crazy to you I felt that it was the right thing to do.'

Gabrielle hesitated, then sat down abruptly, her grey eyes stormy. 'I can't imagine anything which will convince me of that!'

'Then all I can do is ask you to listen to me. Over the past two years or so, Gabrielle, I have become increasingly worried about the life you've been leading. It seemed such a very shallow sort of existence when you have so much potential. I was afraid that unless something was done you would carry on that way, drifting from one entertainment to another, and yet never really finding fulfilment in any of it. Am I right?'

Gabrielle nodded, somewhat shocked at Henry Marshall's accurate assessment. The old man smiled, patting her hand. 'I know you very well, Gabrielle. You're a lot like me in so many ways. You have a fine brain and you need to use it, not let it go to waste on a life where the most taxing decision is whether to buy St Laurent or Chanel. I also knew that, being so like me, you would bitterly resent my interfering.'

Gabrielle gave a small smile. 'Well, at least you admit that part of it is *your* fault!'

'Oh, I do. I decided that something must be done and I had been pondering about what ever since I retired from the firm, but it wasn't until I happened to meet Doyle that I hit upon the right idea.'

She stiffened at the mention of Doyle's name, turning away so that her grandfather couldn't see what she knew must lie in her eyes. 'I see. So this was all his idea, then?'

'Partly. We got to talking about you one evening and I told him that I wished there were someplace I could take you, away from everything, somewhere you would get the chance to put your life into perspective—but where? The world has shrunk over the past few years; there's barely anywhere left where tourism hasn't made its mark. Then Doyle mentioned the rainforest. Even that is being eaten away by man at an alarming pace but there are vast areas of it untouched. It seemed to me possibly one of the few remaining places where you could be alone, take stock, and maybe see that you're wasting your life.' He paused and studied her steadily. 'I love you a great deal, darling. I only wanted the best for you. Perhaps I went about it the wrong way, I don't know, but it was done with the very best of intentions.'

'Oh, Grandpa!' Gabrielle's eyes filled with tears. She leant forward and kissed the old man on the cheek, then drew back and sniffed. 'I suppose it does make a certain kind of sense now that you've explained it to me. You are right, of course. My life was drifting away; I'd started to realise it myself, and now...'

'Now?' he prompted.

'Now I don't think I shall ever be so careless or so wasteful of what I have again. Being in the jungle seemed to concentrate all the vague feelings that something wasn't right. It changed me.'

'That's exactly what Doyle said.'

'Did he?' She jumped up to walk across the room, then walked back again. 'He didn't seem to have a very high opinion of me, if you want the truth.'

'Perhaps that can be partly attributed to what I told him about you. However, I think he now realises, as I did, that you're a strong and capable woman in your own right. In fact, he——' Henry Marshall broke off as the maid tapped on the door and informed him that there was a gentleman waiting in the hall to speak with him. He turned to Gabrielle, smiling. 'That should be the engineer from the mine. He was due to bring me a report on what progress has been made.'

'Then you really are serious about this new project, Grandpa?'

'Of course.' He stood up. 'We can all change our lives any time we choose, darling. We're all masters of our own fate.'

Are we? Gabrielle thought. She watched the door close as her grandfather left the room then walked over to a table set with an array of bottles and poured tonic water into a glass. She took a sip, letting the bitter coolness of the drink ease the dryness from her throat as she pondered upon what her grandfather had just said. If she'd had the chance to choose, would she have *allowed* herself to fall in love with a man who obviously cared nothing at all about her? Of course she wouldn't!

A bitter kind of sadness filled her and she took another swallow of the drink but found she had lost the taste for it now. Setting the glass back on the tray, she turned to go, then stopped abruptly when the door opened and Doyle suddenly appeared. For a moment it felt as though the whole world had ground to a halt, held there by a force greater than any it could create. Then Doyle took another step into the room and closed the door quietly behind him and everything fell back into its rightful place—here and now, Doyle and her, and the coldly cruel way he had deceived her!

'You look little the worse for your adventures, Gabby.'

Gabrielle's heart lifted at the familiar sound of his voice and she turned to pick up the discarded glass, afraid of letting him see how she felt just then. 'I shall take that as a compliment, although I'm not entirely sure it was meant as such. So thank you, Mr Doyle.' She lifted the glass aloft in a mocking acknowledgement, watching the way his mouth thinned. She took a small sip of the water, then had to force herself to swallow it against the knot of pain forming in her throat. 'I could return the compliment, in fact, because you too look little the worse for our stay in the wild.' She let her eyes skim from the top of his damp, dark hair, over his freshly shaved jaw and down his muscular body clad in fresh khaki shirt and trousers. She ached at the pain she felt at seeing him standing there like that, so close, yet so untouchable now. 'But there again you did have an advantage over me, didn't you? You knew all along that our little adventure would have a happy ending.'

He walked towards her, stopping a few feet away, his pale eyes level as they met hers. 'Yes, but that didn't make it any the less taxing, Gabby.'

She had the feeling that he wasn't speaking about the arduous nature of the journey and her eyes flashed with anger. 'Then I suggest that you go into training for the next time and build up your resistance a bit. I would hate to think of any other poor little rich girl going through what I did!'

He had her in his arms before she could think, his eyes blazing down into hers. 'And what's that supposed to mean, honey?'

'You can put any interpretation you like on it. Now, let me go! I imagine you've earned your money now, Doyle, and there aren't any more free bonuses!'

He swore roughly, his hands fastening tighter around her shoulders so that she wanted to cry out at the pain he was inflicting, but pride forbade that she should show such weakness. 'You never learn, do you? You keep on pushing and pushing until you push too far.'

'Oh, but that's where you're wrong.' She smiled sweetly up at him. 'I think you underestimate me. I always learn from my mistakes and *never* repeat them!'

'And last night was a mistake?'

'Of course.' Gabrielle tossed her head so that her hair swung around her shoulders, rich and heavy. 'In normal circumstances I would never have dreamt of such a thing, but what we have been through recently can't be classed as normal, at least not for me!'

'So the mistake was made due to force of circumstance? Is that what you're saying?' His voice had dropped, holding a faintly dangerous note which made a shudder inch slowly up her spine, but Gabrielle forced herself to reply firmly.

'Naturally. What else can it be attributed to?' She gave a soft little laugh, hating to hear the falseness of it. 'Surely you don't imagine that I fell madly in love with you, Doyle?'

He laughed just as softly, but there was nothing but steel in the hard stare of his pale eyes. 'No, I don't imagine that for a moment, Gabby. However, I do know that last night wasn't merely the result of circumstance; neither was what happened this morning.'

Her heart bumped painfully fast, beating a wild tempo of pain and panic which made her whole body shake with its force. 'I have no idea what you're talking about, but then you always have been exceptionally good at riddles.'

'It isn't a riddle; it's perfectly simple. I wanted you and you wanted me. It was desire, Gabby, not circumstance.'

She didn't think she could take much more of this. How could he sum up the pure magic of their lovemaking in such a coldly clinical way? She had *wanted* him, wanted him as she had wanted no other man, but the desire she'd felt had been born out of love, not just some sort of physical reaction!

She pushed against his shoulders to break the hold he had on her, her face filled with contempt. 'Well, I'm so pleased that you've managed to find such a perfect explanation for it. Thank you, Doyle. You really do earn every penny of the fee you're paid, don't you? Not only do you act as guide and protector, even tutor about the environment, but you are also adept at psychology!'

'If you have any other explanation, let's hear it, honey. I'm willing to listen.'

She turned her back on his mocking face, willing herself to remain calm. One careless word too many and that cold, sharp brain of his would start searching for other explanations, more answers, and that was something she didn't want to happen...ever! She had made a fool of herself over a man who cared nothing for her and she wouldn't make herself an even bigger fool by letting him know how she felt.

Walking over to the window, she feigned interest in the view, using the few seconds it gave her to draw on every reserve of strength she had. 'I have no other explanations. Frankly, Doyle, I would prefer to forget that it ever happened, but I suppose it's too much to expect you to act the gentleman.' She glanced round at him, one delicate brow arching. 'So how much will it cost me to ensure your...discretion?' She laughed huskily, watching the dawning anger flickering in his silver eyes. 'I think I was wrong before. There could be another bonus for you to earn, so name your fee, Doyle.'

There was a moment when she thought he was going to come straight across the room and hit her, so great was the fury she saw etched on the lean planes of his face. Then without a word he swung round and left the room, closing the door just as quietly as he had opened it before. And it seemed to Gabrielle that a door had just been closed on her life.

It was impossible to sleep on the soft bed. Gabrielle had grown used to the hardness of the forest floor, to the feeling of space that sleeping in the open had afforded. She tossed restlessly as the night slipped away, then just before dawn could stand it no longer.

Tossing back the smooth cotton sheets, she got up, took her robe from where she'd left it draped over the end of the ornately carved bed and slipped it on, drawing the pale cream stain around her as she quietly left the room. The house was silent in the pre-dawn hour and her bare feet made no sound on the smooth, polished-oak floors as she slipped through each empty room. Over dinner last night her grandfather had told her that he employed half a dozen servants to run the house, sheepishly admitting that half that number would be sufficient but that as they needed the jobs so desperately he hadn't had the heart to dismiss them when he had taken the ranch-house over from its previous owner. Now all those servants were safely asleep in their beds; only Gabrielle was awake at this hour.

There were French doors in the huge sitting-room, giving access to the terrace which ran the length of the front of the house, and on a sudden impulse she opened them and went outside. The air was cool and sweet, far less humid than it had been in the jungle, and for several long minutes she just stood and breathed it in, wishing that its sweet freshness had the power to dim the ache inside her. Her eyes closed, holding back the tears she didn't want to fall. They wouldn't help; nothing would. She loved Doyle, and although she could cry and rail against the cruelty of fate for the hand it had dealt her it wouldn't make any difference to her feelings or to his. All she had ever been to him was a job, a means to earn money.

The grass was wet on her bare feet as she stepped off the paved terrace, but Gabrielle was barely aware of it, or of the fact that the wetness was soaking into the trailing hem of her nightgown and robe. She had no idea where she was going as she started to run across the sweeping lawn. She wasn't running to anything but away from the pain which was tearing her apart, but no matter how hard she tried she couldn't leave it behind. It was part of her now, deeply embedded in her heart and soul. With a tiny moan of distress she slumped to the ground and lay there.

'Gabby! For heaven's sake, what's wrong? Are you ill?'

The deep voice seemed more dream-like than real— in fact it had to be a dream, because Doyle had left the house shortly before dinner the night before. Gabrielle had been in her room and had heard the sound of a car engine. Some instinct had drawn her across to the window just in time to see Doyle driving the Jeep down the curving driveway. He was leaving without bothering to find her to say goodbye and the realisation had been just one more agony to add to all the others. But now her aching heart must have conjured up this image of him, created in her mind what she could never have in reality.

'Gabby, what is it?'

He sounded so real that Gabrielle's hand reached out towards the sound of his deep voice, her fingers searching to touch and feel an insubstantial image, but what they

found was warm, living flesh. Her eyes flew open, shock
glimmering in their depths, her mouth parting on a soft
gasp. 'I ... I thought I had imagined you.'

Doyle caught her hand, holding it between both of
his, the warmth of his flesh seeping into her cold skin.
'I'm no dream, Gabby. I'm far too real to be a dream.'
He lifted her hand and laid it against his cheek to let
her feel the warmth, the faint roughness of his skin where
his beard was darkening his jaw. Gabrielle drank in the
sight of him, unaware of how expressive her face was in
the soft morning light as the sun rose with silent
splendour. Long rose-gold trails of light slid across the
dark sky, making the drops of water clinging to the grass
glitter like diamonds and setting a halo of fire around
Gabrielle's chestnut hair.

Reaching out, Doyle lifted a long, heavy strand and
let it ripple through his fingers, his eyes holding hers.
'If anyone looks like part of a dream then it's you,
Gabrielle. You look far too beautiful to be real.'

His deep voice held a note which made her breath
catch, made her pulse leap to sudden, shocking life. 'But
I am real, Doyle. Just flesh and blood, a woman like
any other.'

His hand slid to her cheek, smoothing the soft skin
which the dawn had turned pearly. 'No, not like anyone
else, sweet. No other woman could sit there and make
me want to forget things I should never forget, think
things I have no right to think.'

'And what if I gave you the right to think them? How
would that change everything?' Her voice was low but
Doyle heard it, his face tightening into lines of strain
which made Gabrielle want to reach out and hold him,

tell him that it didn't matter what happened in the future, rather than cause him pain.

'We can't change anything, Gabby. You are who you are. We come from different worlds.' His voice was flat but it sparked her anger.

'Perhaps, but we managed to share the same world fairly successfully for the past few days, even allowing for the fact that you must be the most stubborn man it has ever been my misfortune to meet!'

'We shared "the same world", as you put it, because we had to. There was no other option.'

'But back in our usual worlds we would make different choices? Is that what you're saying?'

'Adversity makes strange bedfellows, Gabby.' His tone was cynical enough to make her want to hit him. She curbed the urge.

'Is that a fact? How interesting. Yet another of your theories, Doyle?' She tilted her head back, her mouth curved into a taunting smile. 'So it wasn't desire after all which made us share a bed, but good old adversity?'

'Don't push your luck too far, Gabby, or you might regret it.'

There was a warning note in Doyle's voice but Gabrielle chose not to heed it. 'I regret a few things which have happened recently but annoying you isn't one of them. If you want the truth it gives me immense pleasure to dent that iron façade just a little.' She scrambled to her feet, smoothing the damp folds of silk around her slender body as she stared down at Doyle with a mocking tilt of her brows. 'Why did you come back this morning? I thought you'd left last night.'

He got up too, easing his limbs from their cramped position to stand towering over her, just a shade too close for comfort, but she refused to back away. 'How on earth could I leave without saying goodbye to you, Gabby? No, I merely went to pick up a few things I need for the flight back.' He shrugged, drawing her gaze to his powerful shoulders under the familiar khaki covering, and time slid back before she abruptly forced her mind away from what had happened in the jungle. 'It took longer than I expected it to. I got back just a short while ago and as I was getting out of the Jeep I saw you go flying across the lawn as though a thousand devils were after you.'

Her face coloured at the memory of her hasty flight and what had caused it and she glanced away, then heard Doyle laugh softly. 'What were you running from, Gabby?'

'Nothing.' She opted for attack to defend herself from his curiosity. 'Anyway, are you sure that you didn't have another reason for coming back to the house, Doyle? One far more important than a mere desire to say your goodbyes?'

'Obviously you think I have, so name it.'

'Money. After all, we hadn't agreed on the fee I was to pay you for your guaranteed silence about our affair, although perhaps affair is too grand a name for it.' She smoothed a hand down the folds of her robe again, then glanced back at him. 'I'm prepared to be generous, especially as you're such a talented lover. So work something out and let me know how much it is after breakfast.' She turned to walk back to the house but got no further than a couple of steps before Doyle caught her arm and swung her back.

In the misty light his face was dark with anger, his body rigid as he drew her to him and held her there with a steely arm around the back of her waist. 'I ought to tan your backside, lady, for that!'

Gabrielle tossed her head, her own anger soaring to meet and match his, fed by her pain. 'Try it, Doyle! Just try it and see how far you get.'

She spat the challenge at him, daring him to take her up on it, then saw the very instant when his fury changed to something else, and knew in her heart that this was the real reason why she had goaded him. When his head came down and he took her lips with a hungry, forceful demand she made no attempt to evade the kiss but returned it, her hunger matching his step for step. His whole body went rigid as he felt her response, his hands biting into her flesh. He drew back and stared at her, but Gabrielle met his burning gaze proudly.

'It's still there, isn't it, honey? Still just as hot, just as sweet!' His voice grated with emotion, the words bitten out just an instant before he took her mouth again, requiring no answer other than the response her body gave. When he bent and swept her up into his arms to carry her back to the house Gabrielle clung to him, knowing that despite everything this was what she wanted more than anything. It would change nothing, of course. Doyle would go back to his life and she to hers but she would have this last sweet memory to cling to. One beautiful memory to see her through all the long, lonely years.

CHAPTER NINE

'DARLING, you should rest more!'

'I shall do, once tonight is over.' Gabrielle turned to smile at the woman who was watching her with concern. 'Honestly, Mummy, there's no need to worry so. I'm feeling fine, perfectly healthy and...'

'And four months pregnant,' Veronique Marshall added drily. She sighed when she saw Gabrielle's mouth firm. 'I know, women don't need to be treated like invalids just because they're going to have a baby. I did manage to produce you, darling, and although it was some years ago now I can remember what it felt like. The difference is that I had your father to look after me and make sure that I didn't overdo things. I shall never forgive your grandfather for allowing this to happen!'

Gabrielle put down her pen. 'You can't keep blaming Grandfather. It wasn't his fault that I fell in love, Mummy. This child is the result of that and I don't regret it, even though it isn't what I would have chosen to happen.'

'I know, I know.' Veronique sat down on the sofa, crossing her elegant legs in their sheer black stockings. At forty-six she was an older version of Gabrielle, having the same delicate features, the same rich chestnut hair which owed little to any artificial colourants. 'I just wish that you... well, that you would agree to our contacting this man to let him know.'

'What for?' Gabrielle asked bluntly. 'He wasn't in love with me; I've told you that. And I don't intend that he should be pushed into doing the "right thing". The baby is my responsibility. I chose to have it.'

Veronique looked momentarily discomfited. She had been horrified when Gabrielle had first told her about the baby and the circumstances whereby it had been conceived. She had implored her daughter to consider having the pregnancy terminated, but Gabrielle had been adamant in her refusal.

Her emotions had swung from shock to disbelief when she had first discovered that she was pregnant and there were still times when the enormity of it all threatened to overwhelm her. But one thing she had known from the first moment she had suspected that she could be having a baby was that she would never do anything to harm it. As she had quietly explained to her mother and grandfather, she loved Doyle and would love his child too. There was no question of her not having the child. Any fears she had and any tears she shed were hidden in the privacy of her own room while she faced the world with a quiet resolve.

'I'm well aware of that, darling. But sometimes I wonder if your refusal to tell the baby's father isn't something you might come to regret in a few years' time. After all, how are you going to explain to the child what happened, why he or she doesn't have a father like his friends?'

There was sadness on Gabrielle's face as she got up and came around the desk. 'I shall tell him the truth—that I loved his father very much and that's why I wanted to have him so much. This baby is a part of Doyle, the

only part I shall ever have, and I will love it with all my
heart.'

'Oh, Gabrielle, darling!' Veronique got to her feet,
her eyes misting as she hugged her daughter warmly. 'I
wish it could have worked out differently for you. You've
been so brave about it all. What happened in Brazil has
made you grow up, and I don't just mean because you're
expecting this child. You've worked so hard in the past
few months, taking charge of the firm's charitable trust.
I mean, who would have imagined that you could
manage to get tonight's ball all arranged in such a short
time? I am so very proud of you, darling, and I know
that Grandpa feels the same way.'

Gabrielle kissed her mother's smooth cheek and
smiled. 'There were times when I didn't think I would
manage it but...' She shrugged as she walked back to
the desk and picked up a long typed list, automatically
checking through it as she had done several dozen times
already. Tonight's event was the culmination of a great
deal of hard work and planning. Over five hundred
guests were expected to attend the ball at one of
England's most elegant historic houses. Cocktails and
dinner would be followed by dancing to music from one
of the top bands in the country, who had agreed to waive
their usual fee after much gentle persuasion from
Gabrielle. Tickets were expensive but the whole event
had been given so much publicity, thanks to her determination to make the ball a success, that people had
been clamouring to buy them. And every penny of profit
would go to a charity aimed at helping children
throughout the world.

She put the list down again and sighed. 'Well, I doubt there's anything else I can do now. If I've forgotten something vital then it's just too bad.'

'I'm sure it will go beautifully. And once it's over promise me that you'll try to rest a bit more.'

'I shall. Don't worry, Mummy. I shall do everything the doctor orders because I want this baby to have the best start possible.'

'It already has that, Gabrielle. It has you as its mother.'

Veronique patted Gabrielle's cheek, then left the room. Once she had got over her initial shock, her mother had been marvellously supportive and Gabrielle was grateful to her. Yet she knew that her decision not to tell Doyle bothered Veronique as much as it did her grandfather. However, both of them had been forced to accept that it was Gabrielle's right not to do so.

Walking over to the window, which gave a view over the busy London square, Gabrielle let her hand rest lightly on the faint swell of her stomach, feeling the stabbing pain she always felt when she thought about Doyle. She hadn't seen him again since that morning when he had carried her back inside the ranch-house. They had made love then with a depth and intensity which made her blood quicken even now, just to re-member it. But afterwards Gabrielle had lain silently in the bed and watched him dress, knowing that it was the end of whatever relationship they'd had. She had wanted desperately to say something then, to tell him that she loved him and make him stay with her... But in the end she'd said nothing because no words seemed adequate. She loved him so much but he didn't love her, and there was no escaping that. So instead she had remained silent and watched him walk out of her life for good.

Closing her eyes, she summoned up a picture of him in her mind, unsurprised to find the image clear and sharp as though it had been hours, not months since they had parted. Each hard line of his face and the silver-blue shimmer of his eyes were imprinted on her heart like a painting which neither time nor distance could fade. Did he ever think about her or had he put her completely out of his mind? She had no idea but sometimes she felt she would go mad with thinking about him, longing for him. He haunted her dreams each night and would have filled her days if she hadn't thrown herself into the work she was doing for the trust. But was her mother right to say she should tell him about the baby, *his* child?

For a moment Gabrielle savoured the idea with a greedy urgency, imagining what it would be like to find Doyle and speak to him again. Then slowly she forced herself to face up to what she knew: Doyle didn't love her. He had made that plain and to use the baby as an inducement would be a mistake. Far better to spend the rest of her life alone than to force him into a commitment that he would only resent and hate her for.

The music faded and the couples on the dance-floor clapped enthusiastically. Gabrielle looked round, feeling immense satisfaction that it was all going so well. Every fraught moment had been worth it.

There was a soft roll of the drums and the bandleader stepped towards the microphone. 'Ladies and gentlemen, may I now present to you Miss Gabrielle Marshall?'

Gabrielle took a deep breath and ran her hand down the full skirt of her grey shot-silk ballgown. It had been made specially for her and the skilful cut hid her pregnancy from all but the most discerning eye, focusing attention on her creamy smooth shoulders above the strapless bodice and the ripe swell of her breasts. She had swept her heavy chestnut hair to one side and clipped it with a pearl comb so that it fell over one shoulder and put tiny pearl-drop earrings in her ears. She looked beautiful, she knew, even though the one person in the whole world she longed to hear tell her that was miles away.

Pushing thoughts of Doyle to the back of her mind, she mounted the steps to the stage and smiled round at the people who were applauding enthusiastically. Many of them she knew, some were strangers, but all had contributed to making this night more successful than she could ever have dreamed.

'I would just like to thank you all for coming tonight. As you know, the intention of holding this ball was to raise money and I'm sure you will all be delighted to hear that something in the region of fifty thousand pounds will shortly be sent to our chosen charity. So all I can say is thank you. The money will be used to help many needy children.'

There was another round of applause and a few cheers. Gabrielle smiled around the room, then felt all the blood drain from her face as her eyes met a pair of silver-blue ones. For a moment which seemed to verge on eternity she stood and stared at Doyle, then abruptly came to her senses. Stumbling in her haste to escape, she stepped down from the platform, but it was impossible to get away when every few steps someone stopped her to offer their congratulations. When a hand touched her arm she had no need to turn to know whom it belonged to.

'You seem to have achieved a great deal in a short time, Gabby.'

Her eyes flew to his, then skittered away again; she was afraid that if they lingered he would see everything she was feeling, all this heady, crazy joy mingled with fear. Did he know about the baby? Had someone . . . no, not *someone* . . . had her mother or her grandfather told him? Was that why he had come?

She glanced at him again, wishing she could tell, but instead of concentrating on trying to find out how much he knew all she could think of was how marvellous he looked, his dark hair sleek and well-groomed, his powerful physique shown to advantage by the elegant, perfectly tailored evening clothes. The smooth black fabric of his jacket emphasised his broad shoulders and narrow waist, the crisp white shirt highlighted his tanned skin, and Gabrielle drank in the sight of him like a thirsty man offered water in the desert.

'Cat got your tongue, Gabby? It isn't like you to be so quiet. Surely you aren't surprised to see me, not when you sent me the ticket especially so that I would be here?'

His deep voice held a thread of amusement; it slowly filtered through the confusion and shock in her mind. 'Ticket? What do you mean? I didn't send you any ticket, Doyle!'

He cast a quick glance over his shoulder, drawing Gabrielle's attention to the fact that they were standing in the middle of the dance-floor with couples circling them, and attracting a great deal of interest into the bargain. When Doyle slid his hand under her arm and guided her off the floor she made no attempt to break away until she realised that his intention was to lead her right out of the room.

Desperately she tried to ease her arm from his grip but his fingers merely fastened a shade tighter around her as he carried on walking, taking her with him as he strode along the hall. Turning the handle on one of the huge mahogany doors, he glanced inside the room, then thrust Gabrielle before him and closed the door.

'What do you think you're doing? Really, Doyle, you can't just come in here pushing your weight around like this! Now please get out of my way. I have guests to attend to.'

He merely arched one thick brow, leaning back against the door and folding his arms across his chest with a lazy indolence. 'I'm sure your guests will manage without you for a short while. Now, what do you mean you didn't send me the ticket?'

'Exactly that. I have no idea who did, but it wasn't me!'

'And you expect me to believe that?'

'Frankly I don't care what you believe! Why should I want you here? Tell *me* that!'

He took a slow step away from the door, smiling slightly when he saw her take an involuntary step back. 'So that I could see for myself what a success you have made of this venture and be forced to admit that I was wrong about you?'

'I'm not fool enough to imagine that you would ever change your opinion of me, Doyle!' Pain lanced through her and she looked away so that he couldn't see how hurt she felt at this reminder of how he viewed her and her lifestyle.

'I might have to change it. As I said, you seem to have achieved a great deal in a very short time, Gabby. But why have you done it? You could have stepped right back into your old life, concentrated on enjoying yourself again, yet you've chosen to devote your energies to the Marshall Trust.'

'I . . .' She stopped, wondering how to explain in a way he might believe why she'd felt a need to do something positive with her life once she'd got back. 'I think it was seeing that little boy we helped nurse. It brought it home to me how many more such children there must be throughout the world who need help. When Grandpa suggested that I might like to take over the running of the trust now that he has retired it seemed the perfect opportunity to do something.'

'So Henry was right, Gabby. He said that all you needed was some time to get your life together, free from any distractions.'

'But I'm sure he never expected me to find the sort of distractions I found with you, Doyle!' Her hand flew to her mouth just a shade too late to hold back the rash words. But instead of the cutting reply she expected to hear Doyle's voice held a note of regret which was infinitely worse.

'It was never planned, Gabby. I know saying that won't change what happened, but it is true. I've felt guilty as hell ever since.'

She loved him, but all he felt was regret and guilt! Her grey eyes were stormy as they met his pale ones, anger tinting her pale cheeks with a soft rose. 'Don't concern yourself too much about it. It's over and done with now. All part of life's learning experiences.'

'Is it?' He moved closer to her, so close that she could feel the warmth of his body, smell the faint tang of soap on his skin, and her pulse went wild at his closeness. 'Is it really so easy to just shrug it off? Hasn't it left its mark on you, Gabby?'

If only he knew! Unconsciously her hand strayed to her stomach before she snatched it away, terrified that Doyle would somehow sense her secret in that strange way he seemed to understand so much about her. Now more than ever she had to keep the baby a secret from him. She didn't want him to be forced through guilt to make a commitment to her.

'It was something that happened, Doyle. No more, no less than that.'

His eyes narrowed, his mouth thinning in a way which made her feel suddenly uneasy. 'So the sophisticated Miss Marshall was able to take the loss of her virginity in her stride, was she? It was just another of life's little events, like a trip to the doctor or the dentist, something to get over and done with because being a virgin can be inconvenient sometimes?' He laughed with cool contempt. 'Do you find it less of a handicap now, Gabby, to have had some experience? I mean, you've finally taken the plunge, so why not just enjoy the swimming?'

'How dare you?' Her hand arced through the air but it didn't have a chance to connect with his mocking face before he caught it, twisting it sharply behind her back as he hauled her to him.

'A bit too close to the truth, was it, honey? I think all your gentlemen friends should thank me for finally letting loose your inhibitions.'

'I haven't got any gentlemen friends . . . not in the way you mean, Doyle!'

'No? I find that hard to believe.'

'Then I suggest you try harder!'

'So what you are saying in fact, Gabby, is that since you got back you haven't slept with another man?'

'Of course not!'

'I see.' There was something in his voice which made her search his face, but she couldn't really put her finger on what it was. A trace of satisfaction—even *need*? But that was ridiculous. Doyle was merely baiting her as he always did!

She twisted her arm to break his hold, but although he freed her his hands slid to each side of her waist and held her in front of him when she would have moved away.

'Why not, Gabby?'

'I... That's none of your business!' She glared at him, trying to ignore the way her heart gave a sudden alarming little lurch. Why was Doyle doing this, asking these questions?

'Oh, I disagree. I think it is my business. After all, I have a vested interest in your love-life.'

'That... that's ridiculous! What I do is none of your concern.' She laughed bitterly. 'You made it more than plain that you didn't care anything at all about me, Doyle!'

His eyes narrowed, his hands tightening just a fraction so that she could feel the steely strength of his fingers at her waist. 'You were a virgin until we made love, Gabby. I care about that and about how our lovemaking might have affected you.'

So it was all down to guilt—all the questions, all this unexpected interest. Pain was swift and sharp, but no sharper than what she had lived with all these months. 'So what do you want me to say, Doyle? That making love to you was such an earth-shattering experience that

no man could ever follow in your wake? Or is it more
a case of having tasted passion I find that I can live
without it perfectly well? I imagine that's closer to the
truth!'

'So what you're telling me, Gabby, is that you didn't
enjoy what we shared. Is that right?' There was a hard
edge in his deep tones which held danger, but Gabrielle
was too upset to hear it. He had hurt her so much and
now all she wanted to do was hurt him too.

'Yes!'

'You are either a complete liar, sweet, or time has
dimmed your memory. But there is an easy way to decide
which it is.' Almost before she could guess his intention,
he drew her to him, his hands smoothing up her back
to skim across the bare skin above the low-cut bodice
of her dress in a touch which sent an instant surge of
sensation winging through her. Gabrielle held herself
stiffly, trying to force the sensations away, but each
slowly seductive sweep of his hands across her skin
worked a kind of magic on her, sapping her strength,
making her long only to respond to him.

'Don't. Please don't do this, Doyle.' Her voice held
an unconscious plea and her eyes filled with it as they
met his and held in a look which seemed to make time
stand still.

'Why not, Gabby? Because you hate me to touch you
so, or because being held like this is something you want
so much that it scares you?'

Her heart leapt at his choice of words, at the understanding she sensed lay beneath them. Did Doyle know
how she felt about him? Did he sense that she loved him
and that even this gentle touch of his hands was both a
torment and a pleasure? 'Doyle, I...'

He stopped her with a finger against her lips, his eyes silver flames which burned straight through to her soul. 'Don't lie. There's no point when I can so easily prove it one way or the other.'

He bent and kissed her, lightly at first then with a growing hunger designed to overcome her resistance. Gabrielle pushed against his chest, trying desperately to make him stop while she still had the strength to do so, but Doyle was far too strong for her efforts to make any impression. He drew her closer, trapping her hands between them so that her palms were pressed against the warm, hard muscles and she felt the surge his heart gave, felt the way its beat quickened, and she was lost. This was Doyle who held her, Doyle... the man she loved.

Her lips clung to his, warm and tender, giving him the response he sought and so much more. Could he feel how she felt, feel the love flowing from her body to his? Tears ran hotly down Gabrielle's cheeks, mingling with their joined lips, an outward show of all the joy and pain loving him made her feel.

'Gabby!' His voice was deep and faintly husky as he whispered her name, his touch achingly tender as he smoothed his hand down her cheek to wipe away the moisture. 'Don't cry. I...' He bent and kissed her again, hungrily, demandingly, as though words were beyond him. Gabrielle kissed him back, her arms twining around his neck as she held him close while all the lonely months fled, erased by the joy she felt to have him with her again.

'Oh!'

The startled gasp echoed around the room just an instant after the door was thrust open. Doyle raised his head to break off the kiss although his hands still lingered unashamedly at Gabrielle's waist. Gabrielle smiled faintly as she felt the possessive hold of his hands, her senses still reeling from the sensuous spell his kiss had woven around her. Slowly she turned to glance at the intruder, then felt a rush of alarm when she recognised her mother. Even as she watched Veronique made an obvious effort to collect herself from the surprise she'd felt at seeing her daughter locked in such a passionate embrace with a total stranger.

'I'm sorry, darling. I was just worried about you. I...I wouldn't have dreamt of intruding if I'd realised you were with someone.'

Gabrielle eased herself out of Doyle's arms, forcing a smile as she made the introductions. 'That's all right, Mummy. I would like you to meet Doyle. You remember me telling you about him, I'm sure—the man Grandpa engaged for his little stunt. Doyle—my mother, Veronique Marshall.'

She tried to keep her voice level, betraying little of the sudden anxiety she felt. Would her mother understand what she was trying to tell her by that coolly casual introduction? Her hands clenched into fists, her breath caught somewhere in her chest as she watched the older woman step forward, hand outstretched.

'Mr Doyle, I must say that it's a pleasure to meet you at last, and a relief!' Veronique smiled brilliantly as Doyle took her hand and shook it, before glancing at Gabrielle with motherly concern. 'I've been so worried about it, but I knew that once you two had a chance to talk and Gabrielle broke the news to you it would all work out.' She laughed gaily, the only sound in the total silence which filled the room. 'I imagine that was what I just interrupted!'

'Mummy!' Gabrielle stepped forward, her only thought to stop her mother from saying anything more. But Doyle was far too quick for her. He stopped her with a hard hand on her arm and a smile on his mouth which didn't reach his eyes.

'News, Mrs Marshall?' he said softly.

'Why, about the baby, of course!' Veronique glanced from him to Gabrielle, her eyes widening when she saw the pallor of her daughter's face. 'Oh! Oh, dear. I think I may have said something I shouldn't.'

Doyle's mouth curled again, his gaze sliding away from the older woman to rest on Gabrielle's shocked face in a look which made a shiver of fear race uncontrollably down her spine. 'Not at all, Mrs Marshall. I think you said something which should have been said an awful lot sooner. Isn't that right, Gabby? Hasn't your mother only performed a task which should by rights have been yours?'

She didn't think she could stand it, didn't think she could stand there and watch the contempt grow in those silver-blue eyes. They seemed to pierce right into her, their iciness filling her vision, blotting out everything else. Gabrielle took a slow, unsteady step towards the door, but for some reason her legs felt heavy, leaden, and the room was spinning around her. With a faint moan she started to crumple and felt arms catch her before she hit the floor, and even through the darkness which was claiming her she knew that it was Doyle who lifted her, Doyle who now had even more reason to hate her than he had had before.

CHAPTER TEN

THE light was making her eyes hurt. Gabrielle turned her head away from the glare from the lamp and heard the soft click as someone switched it off. She kept her eyes tightly shut, hoping in that way to hide from reality a moment longer, but there was no way to change what had happened. It needed to be faced up to, no matter how much the thought scared her.

'Here, take a sip of this. It will do you good.'

She turned to look at Doyle, her eyes meeting his and skittering away again to focus on the glass he held, unable to cope right then with the coldness she could see in their depths. Would he ever forgive her for what she'd done? She doubted it.

Easing herself up against the arm of the sofa she was lying on, she accepted the glass, but made no attempt to drink from it. 'What is it?'

'Just mineral water. In the circumstances it didn't seem wise to give you alcohol.'

Gabrielle flushed at the hardness of his tone. Lifting the glass to her lips, she took a small sip of the cold water, then lowered it again, holding it carefully in both her hands while she studied the patterns it cast on her dress where it caught the light. 'Doyle, I . . .'

'What? Do you want to apologise? Is that it, Gabby? Are you sorry now that somehow you overlooked telling me about the baby?' His voice was bitter. 'Or is the real truth that you're sorry I found out?'

'Yes...no. I mean, I don't know!' She sat up, trying to make him understand, but knew from the set expression on his face that that was going to be next to impossible.

'Oh, I think you do, honey. I think you know exactly how you feel because you had it all worked out, didn't you? You were going to have this baby...*my* child...but not bother to tell me anything at all about it!'

It was no more than the truth but it sounded so much worse said that way; Doyle's voice was echoing with anger and contempt. Gabrielle took a deep breath, then let it out slowly, her hand straying unconsciously to the small bump which was all the sign the baby had made so far of his presence. 'I didn't want to make you feel it was your...your responsibility.'

'Then whose damned responsibility is it?' He swore roughly as he dropped down beside her on the sofa, his large hand covering hers to press it against her body. 'That's my child, Gabby, that you're carrying. How dare you decide to hide that fact from me? Who gave you the right to make such a decision?'

'You did!' Suddenly she too was angry, angry at him, angry at herself, angry at fate, which had made her fall in love with a man who cared nothing for her! 'You walked out of my life that morning in Brazil, Doyle. That was it...*finito*—the end of our relationship! What was I expected to do when I found out I was pregnant? Start scouting South America for you? And how would you have felt about having me turn up with the wonderful news that I was expecting your baby?' She laughed harshly. 'You made no secret of the fact that all you wanted from me was passion and I'm not fool enough to think that that has changed. This baby makes no difference to anything!'

'Doesn't it? You really imagine that I'm going to disappear from your life knowing that you're carrying my child?'

She pushed his hand away. 'Then what do you suggest, Doyle? That we get married and start playing happy families? That's little short of ridiculous!'

'I'm sure it is in your view. After all, you don't need me to provide for you and the baby, do you, Gabby? You have the means to do that all by yourself. I am expendable, but unfortunately for you I intend to stick around!'

That wasn't what she'd meant at all, but perhaps it was better that she let him believe that than discover the truth. If Doyle had loved her then she would have married him tomorrow, but he didn't. But to allow him to make any sort of commitment solely because of the baby was something she couldn't bear.

Her tone was coolly amused when she spoke again— Miss Gabrielle Marshall at her best. 'Don't you think that's carrying things a little too far? Why give up all you've worked for, Doyle, your business and everything in South America, just to play the doting father until the novelty of the new role pales?'

His eyes were glacial, his voice hard with contempt. 'The same way as you're playing the role of mother? Oh, no, Gabby, don't fool yourself into believing that this is just a passing interest.' He stood up and smiled slowly down at her. 'You aren't going to find it easy to get rid of me now, sweet, because you have something of mine. Oh, and don't concern yourself too much about my business. The South American end of it is easily taken care of. Perhaps Henry forgot to mention to you that I have offices here in London as well? I don't have anything approaching the Marshall money, but I'm not quite the pauper you believed me to be, so don't imagine that it will be easy to push me out of this child's life. I intend to play a major part in its upbringing and if you won't allow me to do that then I shall take you to court and make sure that I'm awarded access!'

'But... but can't you see how impossible it's going to be, Doyle? The baby was an accident. We neither of us planned it to happen. It isn't as though you and I are in love with one another.' Her voice shook on the half-lie but Doyle appeared not to hear the emotion in her tone.

'No, but that means less than nothing now. All that concerns me is this child... my child, Gabby. The child you were going to have and tell me nothing about! That's one link between us which can never be broken.'

He turned away to walk to the door, then paused to glance back at where Gabrielle was sitting, stunned by the anger she'd heard in his voice. 'I shall be back, Gabby. Don't think of running away, will you? Because there isn't anywhere in the world you can hide. I would find you no matter where you went.'

'I...' She stopped as he walked out of the room without bothering to wait to hear what she was going to say. Gabrielle lay back against the cushions, feeling the pain tearing her apart at the thought of the coming months, the ensuing years when she and Doyle would meet for the purpose of discussing the welfare of this child they had created. And the bitterest thought of all was imagining how different it could have been if Doyle had loved her.

*   *   *

Time slipped past, days flowing into weeks until a month had passed, and still Doyle continued to treat Gabrielle with a cold contempt which left scars on her heart. He phoned each day and visited her at the London house several times, stopping only long enough to enquire after her health and the baby's progress.

Gabrielle both longed for and dreaded his visits, the stilted, awkward conversations. She loved him so much that she longed to see him, yet each time it was a fresh disappointment, a new pain to add to all the others. His attitude towards her never varied, never showed any sign of softening. She had committed the biggest crime she could have by attempting to keep the baby a secret from him, and there was no easy way she could explain and make him understand why she had done it. Even if he would believe that she loved him, he didn't love her. There was no point in making any revelations and opening herself up to more heartache.

When Doyle arrived one evening Gabrielle was in the sitting-room flicking through a magazine. She'd felt restless and on edge all day, chafing at the restrictions her advancing pregnancy was imposing on her. At almost six months pregnant she was feeling lumpy, self-conscious of her burgeoning figure and unattractive despite the fact that she had dressed with her customary flair in an emerald-green maternity dress which skimmed her body and provided the perfect foil for her rich chestnut hair. Now to look up and see Doyle standing in the doorway looking disturbingly attractive in evening clothes with a black cashmere overcoat over the top was too much.

She tossed the magazine aside with a tight little smile, the glint of battle in her eyes. 'My, my, but don't we look all dressed up tonight? Surely this isn't for my benefit, Doyle?'

He arched one thick brow, advancing across the room to stand towering over where she was sitting. 'No, I can't say that it is.'

Then whose benefit *was* it for? The thought brought a sudden stab of pain along with it and she sat up straighter, trying to ease her aching back against the cushions. 'I'm sure it isn't. Obviously you're on your way out somewhere so please don't be late on my account.' She laughed shortly. 'But, of course, you aren't here to see me, are you? You just want to check up on the baby's progress. Well, rest assured that everything is going just as it should. The doctor is perfectly happy. Now, off you go, Doyle. Don't keep your date waiting!'

He laughed softly as he bent and lifted her face to stare into her eyes. 'No, they're still grey. For a moment there, Gabby, I thought they might just have changed to green to match that very becoming dress you're wearing!'

Her heart flipped foolishly at the compliment even while her temper gave a sudden little surge. 'Don't flatter yourself! It will be a cold day in hell before I'm ever jealous about you and ... and ...'

Why couldn't she make her mouth form the simple word? Was it just the thought which made her suddenly tongue-tied? Gabrielle had no time to work it out before Doyle completed the sentence for her in a tone which held a wealth of meaning.

'Me and another woman? Would you like to know her name, just for interest's sake, of course?'

'No!' She snatched her head away, afraid of what he would see on her face just then. She didn't want to know the woman's name or anything about her, didn't want to start painting pictures in her head of her and Doyle together! 'I am not in the least bit interested in your *affairs*! Now, if you've achieved all you wanted to by coming here then I suggest you leave.'

'When you're obviously upset about something?' He shook his head, the light from the crystal chandelier glinting on his dark hair. 'I couldn't possibly do that, Gabby. Not in your condition.'

His gaze slid to the swell of her stomach and Gabrielle turned away, biting her lip to hold back the sudden tears. Compared to the unknown woman he was planning on going out with she must look a sight with her swollen body, and she was suddenly achingly conscious of it. 'I'll be fine. In fact I shall feel even better once you leave. You only came to check up on how the baby is so now that you know there's no need to stay any longer.'

'Then if you understand my reason for calling, why are you getting upset? What's the matter, honey?' His voice was deep and soft, untouched by the harshness she'd heard in it for so long now, and the tears welled up faster. Gabrielle sniffed and ran her hand across her eyes, then started nervously when a large hand appeared in front of her, holding a spotless white handkerchief. 'Here, use this.'

She shook her head, a sort of fiercely stubborn pride demanding that she refuse. 'No, thank you. I don't want it. I don't want anything at all from you!'

Doyle sighed heavily, sitting down beside her and calmly turned her to face him so that he could dry her eyes with the handkerchief. 'You always were a stubborn woman, Gabby, and you don't change.'

'*I* don't change? Huh, that's great coming from you! Your opinions are written on tablets of stone, Doyle!'

He laughed deeply, running the smooth, cool cotton down her flushed cheeks before thrusting it back into his pocket, yet even then his hand still lingered against her face. 'Pity help this child we have created, then. He's going to be a strong-minded little devil, I'll bet.'

'If he takes after his father...' She didn't bother to finish the sentence, smiling faintly at the thought of a small boy just like Doyle.

'He might be a she, though. A little girl just as wilful as her mother.'

Gabrielle shook her head. 'No, it's a boy. I had some tests done and it's definitely a boy.'

An expression crossed Doyle's face which Gabrielle found hard to define. He got up abruptly and walked over to the window, staring through the dark wintry night across the square which was lit by the street-lamps. There was a tension about him as he stood there, a stiffness to the set of his shoulders under the elegant coat which Gabrielle couldn't understand. Yet when he turned to look at her there was no hint of anything on his face. 'So I'm to have a son, Gabby. A boy who will be born without the right to my name.'

'I... It's just one of those things, Doyle,' she said lamely. 'Neither of us meant this to happen. It just did.'

'Perhaps. But one thing which has puzzled me a lot recently is why you decided to carry on with the pregnancy. After all, you never expected to see me again, did you? So why did you decide to keep this child when it would have been so easy to rid yourself of the inconvenience of having it?'

Gabrielle's hand flew protectively to the child lying beneath her heart. 'I could never have done that!'

'A lot of women do. It's a fact of life nowadays. Yet you chose to keep the baby...my baby. Why, Gabby?'

There was a softness in his voice which made her heartbeat race. Just for a moment Gabrielle stared at him, feeling all her emotions flowing together in one hot, sweet tide. She loved him so much, loved his child because of it. Was it possible that he felt something for her? She searched his face for any sign but there was nothing in the set lines, and hope died just as quickly as it had been born. 'I couldn't have lived with myself if I'd done that.'

'I see. It was a question of principles.'

What a cold summing-up of so many emotions! But then she couldn't expect Doyle to feel as she felt, could she? Gabrielle nodded briefly. 'Yes, I suppose you could call it that.'

'Then perhaps you can understand that I too have principles, and that it goes against every principle I hold to allow my son to be born without my name.'

She stood up awkwardly, watching him as he came back across the room to stop just in front of her, so close that all she had to do was reach out and touch him. Her fingers tingled with the urge but she fought it, afraid that one small, betraying weakness would lead to so many others, and she couldn't cope with the repercussions. 'I don't think there's any choice about that, Doyle.'

'Oh, but there is, a very simple choice. Marry me, Gabby, and then the child will have both a mother and a father.'

Marry him! Her heart seemed to stop at the thought and she closed her eyes to contain a sudden heady joy.

To marry Doyle and have his child would be all and everything she could ever want; but then sanity returned. Doyle didn't want to marry her because he loved her but out of a sense of duty, to give the baby his name, and that was no basis for any marriage.

'No.' Her voice was little more than a whisper which held an aching note of sadness. She opened her eyes and looked back at Doyle while she let all those brief, precious dreams die. 'No, I won't marry you.'

'Do you want our child to be born illegitimate, then? Don't you care what people will say, Gabby?'

'Of course I do! I care about this baby more than anything.'

'Then do something positive for him. Why is it so hard for you to do that?'

'Because we both know it's a crazy idea.' He was playing on her emotions, of course, but she mustn't weaken.

'How is it crazy? We both want the best for the baby, want to give him the best start in life.'

'How can you say it will be for the best, having parents who married simply because they made a mistake? It...it isn't as though we feel anything for each other.' Her voice wasn't quite steady, but if Doyle heard the hesitation he gave no sign.

'We wanted each other once, Gabby. I doubt that has changed. We would have that going for us at least.'

'No!' She'd meant that it wasn't enough, that sex was no substitute for love, but Doyle misunderstood. His face darkened, his eyes silver-blue flames as they held hers.

'Deny it all you like, my sweet, but we both know it's true. No matter what either of us thinks about the other there is still that chemistry. Do you need proof, Gabby?'

He had her in his arms before she could make any attempt to move away, holding her as he stared down into her shocked eyes.

'Stop it, Doyle! This won't solve anything. It's madness!'

He smiled thinly, his hand sliding up her spine to tangle in the thickness of her hair. 'It always was a kind of madness, though. Two people who came together and discovered a passion few find in a lifetime.'

His words made her heart ache. What they had shared had been just that to him—passion—but for her it had been so much more than a pleasure they had found in each other's body. 'It isn't enough to build a marriage on. You must see that.'

He shook his head, his fingers tracing the curve of her skull before sliding down to the nape of her neck to smooth across the warm skin. 'I imagine it's more than a lot of people have, that plus the baby. Can't you remember how it felt, Gabby, to touch and be touched, to feel the fire burning?'

'No, I can't! I don't want to remember, Doyle. It should never have happened. It was a...a mistake!'

His fingers closed around the nape of her neck, tilting her head back. 'Is that how you remember it? Tut-tut, it seems to me that you need a reminder, Gabby, of just how sweet it was.'

'I don't want any reminders! Now, let me——'

She got no further as Doyle bent and kissed her, his mouth swallowing up the heated, desperate words. Gabrielle pushed against him to make him let her go, but although he held her gently it was impossible to break the hold he had on her. With a sensuous thoroughness he plundered her mouth, then skimmed kisses along her jaw before drawing back to smile into her eyes.

'Was that so dreadful, Gabby? Did you loathe every second of that kiss?'

His tone mocked her and she glared at him, caution being tossed aside. 'Yes! I loathed every single second if you——'

Once again she didn't complete the sentence, her mouth once more becoming captive to the mastery of Doyle's. This time, though, the kiss was bolder, even more erotic, as he slid his tongue inside her mouth to tangle it with hers in a primitive dance which lit fires inside her even while she called herself every kind of fool for showing such weakness. All he wanted was to prove a point, but even knowing it didn't stop the blood from beating heavily through her veins, didn't quieten the rapid drumming of her heart. Resistance melted away under the heat of passion, leaving Gabrielle helpless in Doyle's arms, but surprisingly when he raised his head there was no hint of triumph in his glittering eyes, just a calm acceptance that they both now knew the truth.

'Would it be so hard to marry me and share that with me, Gabby? We could build a good life together for our son and find pleasure in one another.'

Gabrielle closed her eyes against the temptation. She couldn't deny that Doyle was right; there was still that wild desire between them, but how long would it last without love as its foundation? How soon would Doyle tire of her once passion faded? She didn't think she could bear the thought of losing him at some point in the future. It was better to remain as she was rather than go through all that heartache.

'No.' She tried her best to hide the agony she felt. If Doyle had spoken one word of love or even affection then it could have been so different, but he hadn't. He was prepared to marry her only because of the baby. 'No, I won't marry you. It would be a mistake we would both regret. Now, I really can't see any point in continuing with this discussion. It's merely a waste of time.'

'Not at all. On the contrary, it's been an education. It's opened my eyes to what you really are, Gabby. It's made me realise that there is no way that I am prepared to allow my son to be brought up by you, not when you're so unwilling to do anything for his benefit.'

'How dare you? Get out.' She took a quick step towards him, but he made no move.

'I'm going but I shall be back, sweet. And I shall keep on coming back until the baby is born and then . . .' He shrugged. In the clear light from the chandelier his face looked even harsher, every line starkly etched. He looked big and tough and uncompromising as he stood there, staring at her so coldly in a way which cut her to the quick. She loved him so much but she only had to see that expression on his face to know how he felt.

'Then . . . what?' she asked with a show of bravado.

'Then I shall do everything in my power to gain custody of the child.'

'What?' Gabrielle stared at him in horror. 'But that's ridiculous! On what grounds? Tell me!'

'That you are an unfit mother. Your jet-setting lifestyle hardly provides a secure environment for a young child, does it? I'm sure it wouldn't look good presented in court, not when I've finished.'

'You're mad. The case would never even reach the courts. It would be thrown out well before that stage and you know it!'

'Are you sure?' He shrugged lightly. 'However, it's a risk I'm prepared to take. The question is, are you prepared to face all the publicity it would cause? Can't you imagine how some of the tabloids would set to work on the story, Gabby? All that background detail of the days we spent alone together in the jungle.' He smiled coldly. 'I wonder how the trustees of the Marshall Trust will view it? Will they be happy that the woman in charge is involved in such an unsavoury scandal? Or will they feel, perhaps rightly, that that kind of publicity isn't what they want for a charity whose aim is to help children?'

Gabrielle couldn't seem to think straight. Her head was whirling with what Doyle had said. Could he really sue for custody? Did he have the right to do that? She wished she could be certain but the law was changing all the time and there had been cases brought to court in recent times which would have been unthinkable a few years ago. And then there would be all the publicity, as he'd said, even if the case was thrown out in the end. Working for the trust had become a lifeline for her and would continue to be one in the future. On sleepless nights she had tried to console herself with the thought that she would have the baby and the work to fill all the empty, lonely hours, but the trustees would take a very dim view of any hint of scandal touching the Marshall name.

'Do you hate me so much, Doyle?' she asked brokenly.

He stared back at her for a long moment, his expression hard to define. 'No, I don't hate you, Gabby. I don't feel anything like hatred for you, in fact. I'm

not an unreasonable man so I'll give you some time to
think over what I've told you before making your final
decision. Marry me and that's the end of it, but don't
make the mistake of thinking that I won't do everything
I've warned you I'm prepared to do if you refuse. The
welfare of my child is too important to me.'

He left, but long after the front door closed Gabrielle
remained where she was. She pressed her hand over the
mound of the baby, feeling the small movements beneath her palm as tears filled her eyes. Maybe Doyle
didn't hate her because all he felt for her was contempt,
and that was somehow worse. It was that contempt which
would drive him to carry out his threats if she wouldn't
agree to marry him, but now more than ever that seemed
like an impossible option. How could she face a future
with a man who felt that way about her? There had to
be another way to work this out and make Doyle see
sense if she just had the time to find it. The one thing
she was certain of was that she would never allow him
to take her child!

CHAPTER ELEVEN

'A LETTER for you, Madame Marshall.'

'*Merci, madame.*' Gabrielle took the letter from the concierge with a smile of thanks, then carried on across the marble-floored foyer to the lift which would take her up to her apartment. She pressed the button to summon it then glanced at the envelope, sighing as she recognised her mother's handwriting. It hardly seemed worth opening it because she already knew what it would contain. Veronique had written the same thing in each one of her letters—pleas for Gabrielle to see sense and return to London. But the trouble was that her mother had no idea what had made her seek refuge in the apartment she was renting in Paris.

She hadn't told her mother what Doyle had threatened to do, hadn't told anyone apart from the solicitor she had consulted for advice. In his view it was 'most unlikely' that Doyle would be awarded custody even if he did succeed in bringing the case to court, but 'unlikely' wasn't the absolute guarantee Gabrielle needed. When Gabrielle had pressed him further he had reiterated her own thoughts—that the law was never cut and dried and that changes were occurring all the time. As for the publicity it could cause, that was open to speculation, but Gabrielle had read enough in the papers to know how intrusive the Press could be, and how damaging. Quite apart from any adverse reactions from members of the

Marshall Trust, there was the child to consider. How would he feel at some later date if he discovered how contemptuous his father must have been of his mother if he'd been prepared to go to such lengths? It was something no child should have to face.

Just facing up to it herself had been a bitterly painful experience for Gabrielle, too painful for her to share it with her mother. So in the end she'd told her nothing, just sworn her to secrecy. Oh, she wasn't foolish enough to imagine that she could hide from Doyle forever, but once the baby was born she would feel better able to cope, more capable of fighting him.

The lift creaked to a stop and Gabrielle pushed open the ornate gilt gate and stepped inside, pressing the button for the third floor. She'd been lucky to find the apartment at such short notice, but then the rent being asked was extortionate, reflecting its central location on the Avenue Victor Hugo. It belonged to some actress or other who used it infrequently when she was in Paris, and its lavishly decorated interior reflected a theatrical taste, with lots of gilt and marble all over the place. However, the rooms were comfortable, if not to Gabrielle's taste, and security total. No one got past Madame Mathieu on the reception desk!

Gabrielle let herself in and kicked off her shoes, wriggling her aching feet into the thick-pile cream rug with a murmur of relief. She'd walked further than she had intended to, avoiding the crowds on the Champs-Elysées and opting for the quieter streets with their exclusive boutiques. With Christmas just a few weeks away there was a bustle about the city, an air of anticipation which had drawn her to wander further and further afield. She had stopped at the ice-cream parlour on the Place Victor

Hugo, taking her time eating the sweet confection she
didn't really want, just to put off the moment when she
had to return to the solitude of the flat and all the memories which lay in wait for her. She might have run from
Doyle but he was never far from her thoughts.

She made coffee while she skimmed through the letter,
smiling wryly as she discovered that she'd been right
about its content. Putting it aside, she filled a cup with
the delicious coffee and carried it into the elegantly
ornate salon, flicking on the lamps as she went. Night
was drawing in and outside the long windows the sky
was turning purplish-black, a few spots of rain spat-
tering against the glass. This was the time she dreaded
most, when day faded and night drew close, the time
when her mind became even more active, filled with
memories of Doyle. How she missed him!

The shrill sound of the house phone steadied her.
Setting the cup down on a small table, Gabrielle hurried
to answer it.

'Madame Marshall, there is a gentleman here to see
you, a Monsieur Marshall. Shall I permit him to come
up?'

Grandfather, here? Gabrielle frowned as she gave per-
mission, hurrying to open the front door. But the man
who stepped from the lift bore little resemblance to
Henry Marshall. For a horror-stricken moment Gabrielle
stared at Doyle's familiar figure, then turned and ran
back inside the flat, but she was just a shade too slow
in closing the door.

With an ease that was galling he pushed it open, setting
Gabrielle aside as he turned and closed it behind him,
then flicked her a sardonic glance. 'Ten out of ten,

Gabby. You've given me a real run for my money finding you.'

Gabrielle stared coldly back at him, ruthlessly quelling the rapid pounding of her heart. All right, so Doyle did look marvellous in those close-fitting jeans which hugged his narrow hips, with an ice-blue sweater which matched his eyes and his dark hair wind-blown across his forehead, but she had to remember what had happened the last time they had spoken, the reasons why she had run away from him. This crazy, helpless response her body gave didn't count for anything!

'If you're expecting me to apologise then hard luck. I didn't go to the trouble of leaving London so that you could turn up on the doorstep the next minute with your nasty threats!'

His eyes narrowed and he took a slow step towards her. 'I would be careful what I said if I were you, honey. I've flown straight here from Brazil and frankly I'm not in the mood for any of your smart remarks.'

'Brazil? Then you saw Grandpa? Did he tell you where to find me?' Her tone reflected her disappointment that Henry should betray her that way, and Doyle gave a thin-lipped smile.

'Not exactly. I just happened to come across a letter you'd sent him on his desk when he was out of the room. I got the address from that.'

'You mean you went through Grandfather's private papers? And then you had the nerve to use his name when you got here. That's despicable even for you, Doyle!'

'Needs must, Gabby. I doubt you would have welcomed me with open arms if I'd given my name to the dragon on guard at the desk downstairs.' He walked past

her into the sitting-room, staring round at the ornate
furnishings with a faint lift of one dark brow. 'Mmm,
obviously I was wasting my time worrying about you,
Gabby. You don't appear to have been suffering too
much hardship since you hid yourself away.'

'Worrying about me?' She smiled bitterly as she followed him into the room, and picked up her coffee more
for something to do with her trembling hands than out
of a desire to drink the cooling liquid. 'Don't you mean
that you were worried about the baby? Well, you can
stop worrying, Doyle. The baby is fine and everything
is just as it should be. Perhaps you would like to see the
doctor's report if you won't take my word for it?'

He swore softly as he came across to her. 'Did you
really imagine that I would just let you disappear,
Gabby?'

She put the cup down, afraid of spilling coffee on to
the pale silk sofa. 'No. I knew you would do everything
in your power to find me.'

'Then why attempt to run away?' He caught her by
the shoulders and held her in front of him, his eyes glittering fiercely. 'I couldn't believe it when I phoned and
your mother told me you weren't at home, that you had
gone away. I went straight round to the house but she
swore she had no idea where you'd gone.'

'She hadn't, not then, because I didn't know myself
where I'd be staying. I just caught a flight to Paris and
found accommodation when I got here. And then I made
her promise not to tell anyone where I was.'

'Anyone? Don't you mean me?' His laughter was
harsh and oddly strained. It seemed to be filled with a
raw kind of pain, but that was ridiculous. Doyle was
granite through to the core and nothing could hurt him!

'Yes! If you want the truth. And can you blame me, Doyle? You threaten to take my child away from me so what do you expect me to do? Stay there and let you carry out all your rotten threats? I won't ever allow you to do it. Do you hear me? You have no right to take my child!' She was shaking now, her whole body consumed by this fear which she had lived with day and night for the past few weeks. But when she tried to twist out of Doyle's grasp he wouldn't let her.

'Why do you care so much about this child, Gabby?' His voice had dropped a note, dark and oddly disturbing now, and Gabrielle felt her senses stir. She looked away from the pale, hypnotic shimmer of his eyes, which were watching her so intently, trying to understand what he was getting at, but her head seemed to be hazy with so many foolish thoughts.

'It's only natural that I should care about it!'

'My child, though, Gabby. You have never made any attempt to deny that, have you? Your mother told me that you admitted it was mine right from the moment you knew you were pregnant.'

'Of course. Why should I lie?'

'Why indeed? It's another mystery to add to the reason why you absolutely refused to consider a termination. Your mother told me that as well.'

Her mother had told him far too much from the sound of it! Gabrielle forced herself to meet his gaze. 'You knew that already. I told you that it wasn't an option.'

'Mmm, you did. It was a matter of principle. Wasn't that it?'

She wished he wouldn't watch her like that. It felt as though he could see inside her head, read things she didn't want him to know about. With a quick twist she managed to break his hold, and walked away from him to sit down on the sofa. 'What is this all about, Doyle?' she asked quietly. 'You're asking questions you already know the answers to. It's just a waste of time.'

'Getting to know one another doesn't seem like a waste of time to me. It's something we should have done a long time ago.'

'When?' She laughed a trifle hysterically. 'We were together just a few days in the jungle and we were hardly concerned with compiling each other's biography! Anyway, you made no attempt to hide how you felt. You knew all there was to know about me, didn't you, Doyle?'

'I thought I did. But somehow I keep adding up all the things I really know and the picture becomes distorted.'

His words made warmth run through her, but deliberately she banked it down. She knew what Doyle felt; she would be a fool to hope for anything different from him.

'What do you expect me to say to that? That you've been wrong about me?' She shrugged lightly. 'Sorry, Doyle, but I've given up trying to change your opinion of me.'

He ignored her sarcasm, sitting down opposite her on one of the huge silk-covered chairs and crossing one long leg over the other. 'And that's why I think we should try to understand one another. You know nothing at all about me, do you, Gabby? Yet you're having my baby. Aren't you interested?'

Of course she was! She longed to learn more about him, ached to hear the details of his life and how it had formed him into the man he was today. But betraying her interest would make her so very vulnerable. She gave a small toss of her head, shaking the length of her hair back over her shoulders as she tried to instil a note of boredom into her voice to hide her curiosity. 'It appears that you want to tell me, so feel free.'

He smiled in a way which made her think he understood only too well how she felt, but made no outright comment. 'Where should I begin? How about right at the beginning? My parents were quite elderly when I was born. I think they had given up all hope of ever having a child and then I arrived on the scene and, I imagine, disrupted their nicely organised life. Suffice it to say that we didn't always see eye to eye, and that when they died within six months of each other when I was seventeen it wasn't the blow it might have been. I was pretty self-reliant by then, used to doing things my way, which was a huge handicap when I first joined the army.'

'The army?' Gabrielle couldn't help her exclamation of surprise.

'Yes. I had never been able to think what I wanted to do and joined on impulse.' He shrugged, running a hand over his dark hair to smooth it back from his forehead. 'I finished up in the SAS with the rank of major.'

Gabrielle didn't quite know what to say. She had only the haziest of ideas what the SAS did, gleaned from what she'd read in newspapers. But she did know that the top commando unit was renowned worldwide for its expertise. It specialised in undercover operations and anti-terrorist activities and the men who joined were the most highly skilled and tough in the British Army. To reach the rank of major Doyle must have been one of the best there was and now that she was getting over her initial shock she wasn't surprised. Look how he had coped in the jungle!

She voiced the thought and saw him smile. 'Yes, jungle training was my speciality, as it happens, although we were trained for any terrain from the Arctic to the desert.'

'Why did you leave?' she asked quietly.

He paused for a moment, as though looking for the right words. 'I think I just realised that I wanted a change, a different kind of challenge. I left the service two years ago and set up this company, using knowledge I had gained from being in the SAS.' He must have seen Gabrielle's bewilderment because he continued, 'It isn't only a freight company I run, although the major bulk of the work concerns that. I also carry people—people who might have difficulty, shall we say, in reaching their destination safely using normal transportation methods?'

Gabrielle shivered as she heard the edge to his deep voice. 'It sounds dangerous work.'

'Not if the risks are understood and any potential problems taken care of. The men I employ are highly qualified for the job so that it makes no difference if the cargo is a million pounds' worth of diamonds or some top diplomat—I can guarantee safe delivery. That's the reputation I have built up in the past two years and it seems that people are prepared to pay and pay well for that kind of service. I shall be expanding into the North American market in the next month and have had enquiries from Japan about setting up there.' He stared levelly at her. 'So now you know just a bit more about me, Gabrielle. A few facts about the man who is the father of that child you're carrying.'

What did he want her to say? That what he had told her surprised her? It did. She had known so little about

Doyle before and now he had filled in so many gaps, yet there were other gaps, even bigger ones. For instance his wife; he had made no mention of her and she longed to ask him but couldn't quite pluck up the courage when she didn't really understand why he had told her what he had in the first place.

When Doyle suddenly stood up she started nervously, but he merely smiled calmly down at her. 'Funny, isn't it, honey? You learn a bit more and then it opens up all sorts of fresh questions.'

So he had done it deliberately, tantalised her with these snippets of information! She glared up at him, then felt her breath catch when he suddenly bent and kissed her hard on the mouth before she had the chance even to think of turning away. When he drew back she touched her burning lips with the tip of a finger, her eyes huge as they flew to his pale ones.

'How will you cope with all the questions our child will ask about his father, Gabby? What will you tell him about me? Do you know enough even now to build a picture of me in his mind and show him life through my eyes?'

'I...' The colour ebbed from her face, taking with it all the warmth the kiss had left behind. 'I don't intend to pretend you don't exist, Doyle. I shall tell him all I know and you will be able to see him yourself and fill in any gaps.'

'Will I? Once-a-week visits in some artificial atmosphere, a weekend father taking the child to the cinema, the zoo?' His face was harsh now, his eyes cutting into hers. 'That isn't enough, Gabby. I want to be with my child, to help bring him up and teach him values. God knows, my own father did little in that respect for me, but I don't intend it to be the same for my son!'

'So what exactly are you saying, Doyle?' Gabrielle got up and faced him, her heart thundering. 'That you still intend to try for custody? Well, I won't let you take my child from me, do you hear? I won't!'

Tension seemed to grip him, his whole body rigid. 'Then you know the answer to it. Marry me, Gabby, and we shall bring up our child together.'

There was a moment, just one, when temptation was so hot and sweet that she nearly caved in and gave him the answer he wanted, but with a superhuman strength drawn from heaven knew where she managed to resist. 'No. It wouldn't work. You know it wouldn't!'

'I don't know any such thing. All I can see is you being deliberately stubborn about something which makes sense. But I think I understand why now, Gabby.'

There was something in Doyle's tone which made her blood stir, her heart leap, her pulse race a shade faster. She drew in a shaky breath, danger seeming to fill the very air between them. 'I have no idea what you mean,' she said curtly.

He laughed, a low sound which ran through every stretched nerve in her body. 'It's all linked in with why you wanted this baby so much, sweet. My child.' He brushed her cheek with his fingertips as he tilted her face to stare quietly into her eyes. 'Think about that, Gabby, and then give me an answer. I'll be waiting.' He moved away from her, feeling in his pocket for his wallet, and dropped a small card on to the table by the sofa. 'You can reach me there any time, night or day.'

'Doyle, I...' She stopped him when he would have left, then found she had nothing to say, no words which would come out of all the confusion in her head. Doyle merely smiled as she fell silent then opened the front door and left the apartment while Gabrielle stared after him with shocked eyes. She sank down on to the sofa, clasping her trembling hands in her lap as she tried to convince herself that she was mistaken, that Doyle had no idea that she was in love with him. But every time she recalled what he'd just said the idea grew stronger.

She loved him and he knew it. Did it make their situation better or worse? She wished she knew because maybe then she would know what to do next!

Gabrielle was in the kitchen drinking coffee when the telephone rang the following morning. She'd spent a near sleepless night going over everything that had happened, but no amount of tossing and turning had produced a solution to her dilemma. Now the sudden ringing of the phone startled her so much that coffee spilled from the cup across the marble counter.

For a long moment she stared at the dark pool, then slowly turned and walked over to the phone, feeling her heart thudding with every slow step she took. It had to be Doyle calling, of course, at this time of the morning. But what was she going to say to him? How could she just admit how she felt? However, when she finally summoned up the courage to answer, she discovered that it wasn't Doyle but Henry Marshall—the real Henry Marshall this time!

'Gabrielle . . . are you all right, darling? I was beginning to get worried when you didn't answer at first.'

'I'm fine, Grandpa. I . . . I just spilled some coffee and was trying to mop it up before it made a dreadful mess,' she lied hurriedly.

'I see. Look, darling, there's no point in my beating about the bush. Has Doyle been to see you?'

'Why, yes. How did you know he was coming here?'

'Because he wouldn't be the man I think he is if he didn't find the letter I carefully left on my desk with your address on it,' Henry said drily.

'Grandfather! You mean you *knew* he would find it? But why——?'

He cut off her shocked protest with a sigh. 'Why did I want him to? Same reason as I sent him that invitation to the ball you arranged. Someone had to do something to get you two stubborn people together!'

'Oh, Grandpa!' Gabrielle didn't know whether to laugh or cry.

'Don't "Oh, Grandpa" me, young lady! I have rarely met two people who are making such a mess of their lives. Granted, I feel more than a bit responsible. If I hadn't brought you both together then none of this would have happened.'

Gabrielle sighed sadly, her voice reflecting how she felt. 'I don't regret it, Grandpa.'

The old man's tone softened. 'I know, but I'm old-fashioned enough to believe that children need both parents. Oddly enough it appears that Doyle feels much the same. He told me that he had asked you to marry him but that you refused.'

'I won't marry him just because of the baby. It wouldn't work.'

'You love him, don't you, Gabrielle?'

'You know I do.'

'Then marry him because of that.'

'But he doesn't love me!'

'How do you know? Darling, Doyle isn't the kind of man who goes around shouting about what he feels. He has led a tough life from what I can gather. Maybe he finds it hard to admit to his feelings.'

Was it possible? For a few tempting seconds Gabrielle toyed with the idea, then dismissed it. 'No. He hates me. He must do because he has threatened to try to gain custody of the baby. That's why I left London so hurriedly.'

'I see. Well, I have my own views why he did that but it's not for me to say. The only bit of advice I will give you, Gabrielle, is that pride is a cold companion to live with. If you love Doyle then take your courage in both hands and find out if he feels anything for you. Don't ruin your life because you're afraid of being hurt.'

Henry said goodbye and hung up. Slowly Gabrielle replaced the receiver, then went and picked up a cloth to wipe up the spilled coffee. Her hand stilled on the counter, her heart tapping out a fast little rhythm which made her feel sick. Was it just possible that Doyle really did care about her but found it impossible to admit to how he felt? He *wanted* her, he'd made no pretence about that, but did he feel anything else? Suddenly she knew that if there was a chance she was going to take it. She was going to find Doyle and tell him how she felt!

The London weather was little better than what she'd left behind in Paris. Heavy rain swept the busy streets, driven by a biting wind which cut through the enveloping folds of her raincoat. The taxi had dropped her off at the gates of the dockside complex and now Gabrielle walked carefully between the puddles until she reached the door she wanted. There was no sign outside the building, nothing to confirm that this was where Doyle had his offices, just a number which matched the one printed on the small card she was clutching in her hand.

She glanced round at the wet tarmac, at the river which ran grey and oily in the fading evening light, and tried to find again the courage which had carried her this far, but it seemed to have deserted her now that she'd reached the end of her journey. How could she just walk in there and declare her feelings and leave herself open to all sorts of pain? She must have been mad even to contemplate it!

Gabrielle half turned to go when the door was suddenly flung open and a man came out, almost cannoning into her. He steadied her in a purely reflex action, concern showing on his good-looking face as he studied her pallor.

'Are you OK? I didn't mean to scare you.'

Gabrielle summoned up a watery smile as she edged away from him. He looked nothing at all like Doyle—slim and blond-haired, although there was a wiry strength about the hands which had steadied her—yet for some reason his manner reminded her sharply of Doyle's. He had the same direct way of looking at her, the same air of command. Heaven help her but she was starting to imagine that every man she met bore a resemblance to him!

'I'm fine, really,' she said quickly. 'It was as much my fault as yours.'

The man smiled easily, but there was an intentness to the look he treated Gabrielle to. 'As long as you aren't hurt. Were you looking for Doyle?'

Gabrielle's heart leapt as her eyes drifted past the stranger to the closed door. So Doyle was there. All she had to do was walk in and . . . and . . . The very last of her courage disappeared like smoke on a wind and she took a hasty step away from the office. 'It . . . it doesn't matter. Really it doesn't.'

'Don't be silly. You've come all this way on a night like this so go on in.' Before she could protest any more the man pushed the door open and ushered Gabrielle inside, then shouted past her, 'Someone here to see you, Doyle.'

'Be right out.'

Panic rose inside Gabrielle at the sound of that familiar voice, but as she turned to leave she found that the stranger was in her way, and then it was too late because suddenly Doyle was in the room.

'Gabby!' His tone betrayed his surprise, every muscle in his body going rigid as he stood and stared at her with eyes which looked like quicksilver, pale and glittering, yet holding something which made heat flow along Gabrielle's frozen veins.

'Mmm, so that's the lie of the land, eh? Want me to stay around, Doyle?'

Gabrielle jumped when the man spoke, barely hearing the light mockery in his tone, but Doyle heard it. His gaze shifted to the other man at once, some of the tension easing from him.

'Get the hell out of here, O'Rourke,' he said without rancour.

'Yes, sir, Major!' The blond man gave a mocking salute then disappeared, leaving Gabrielle and Doyle alone. Gabrielle forced her gaze away from Doyle and looked round the room, taking stock of the pale green walls, the leather chairs grouped around a low coffee-table, more utilitarian than ornamental, the heavy mahogany desk which held an array of office equipment. Two doors led off the room, one of which Doyle had appeared through just minutes before, but if there was anyone else in the building they were being extremely quiet. There seemed to be just her and Doyle alone, and suddenly Gabrielle couldn't cope with the implications of that!

'I'm sorry if I...'

'Are you all right? You...'

Both spoke together, then stopped abruptly. Doyle gave a slight smile then said quietly, 'You first, Gabby.'

Gabrielle gripped her leather bag tighter. 'I was just going to say that I was sorry if I was interrupting anything. That man insisted I should come in.'

'You aren't, and he was right to do so. There isn't a lot of point in your coming here then turning round and going away again.'

Her cheeks burned at the observation and she hunted for something else to say to cover her nervousness. This was worse than she'd imagined! 'Does he work for you... that man, I mean?'

Doyle arched a brow, leaning indolently against the wall and folding his arms across his broad chest. He was wearing black trousers and a thin white cotton shirt with his tie pulled loose and the shirt-sleeves rolled up above his elbows, and he looked so vitally and devastatingly male that Gabrielle's heart was beating itself half to death. 'If you really want to know then the answer is a bit of both, yes and no. He works for me on odd occasions but I don't employ him. He's a free agent. But somehow I don't think you came here to discuss my working arrangements, did you, honey?'

Gabrielle drew herself up and glared at him, hating him for his sarcasm. 'No, I didn't!'

'Then why did you come?' There was no softening to those deep tones, no hint that he was longing to hear her reasons, and Gabrielle played for time while she tried to think.

'Surely you knew I would come? Nothing has been cleared up, Doyle. I want to know what you intend to do after the baby is born.'

'That depends on a lot of things, Gabby.' He glanced around the room then stepped to one side of the door. 'We'd better go into my office. We don't want to be interrupted.'

Gabrielle hesitated only briefly, then crossed the room, keeping her face averted as she passed Doyle. Her eyes slid over the small name-plate screwed to the wooden door and she paused. J.J. Doyle! She didn't even know what Doyle's full name was, and here she was contemplating telling him that she loved him. She must be mad!

'What's wrong, Gabby?'

She turned to glare at him, not realising that he was so close, and felt her pulse leap when her body brushed against his. Annoyed by her reaction, she stabbed a finger at the name-plate. 'This! Do you realise that I don't even know your real name? Crazy, isn't it? I'm having the child of a man whom I know only by his surname!'

Doyle's hands fastened around her shoulders as he moved her gently into the room and closed the door, but even then he didn't let her go. He turned her to face him. 'But love is a kind of madness, isn't it, Gabby? There's no rhyme or reason for why we feel it; it just happens, and plays havoc with our lives. But it's the sweetest kind of madness, don't you think?'

His lips were so warm that they filled her with warmth. It curled into every cold corner of her heart, seeped into every ache and melted it away. Gabrielle clung to him, kissing him back with all the love she felt, and heard him give a rough sigh. 'Why have you come, Gabrielle? Tell me, please.'

Was it the 'please' which made her courage come flowing back, that hint of vulnerability in Doyle's deep voice?

It made no difference why because suddenly the words which had been locked inside Gabrielle flowed freely. 'Because I love you, Doyle. I love you enough to take a chance by telling you how I feel. I love you and that's why I want this baby so much. I...I love you. It's as simple as that.'

There was a moment when time hung suspended, when it felt as though the world held its breath, and then Doyle spoke, his voice husky with emotion. 'And I love you, Gabby. I love you more than I thought it possible ever to love anyone.'

There were tears in Gabrielle's eyes as she went on tiptoe to press her mouth to his, her lips warm and giving as they clung to those of the man she loved. When she slowly drew back she could see the naked emotion she felt reflected in Doyle's eyes, betraying the depth of his feelings for her, and all the fears, all the heartache faded.

He drew her close, cradling her gently against the strength of his body while he stroked her hair, her cheek, her shoulder, as though it was almost more than he could believe that she was here and that he could touch her. 'I was so afraid, Gabby. Afraid that you wouldn't come and that I had misread all the signs. When you disappeared from London I was frantic. I knew that it was my fault, that I'd pushed you too hard.'

'Why did you make all those threats? Would you have gone through with them and tried to take the baby from me?'

'No.' He sighed roughly, his hands tightening on her shoulders. 'I was incensed by your refusal to marry me. I don't think I had fully admitted to myself how I felt about you, hadn't realised that trying to force you to marry me was almost an act of desperation on my part. Then you ran off and I couldn't find you at first. Once I had found out where you were, though, and went to see you everything started to become clear—how I felt, how I hoped you felt. I kept adding it all up in my head to convince myself that I was right to think you might love me, but I knew I had to give you the space to make a decision. Coming back here and hoping and praying that you would follow me has been one of the hardest things I've ever done!'

Gabrielle laughed softly, nestling closer. 'Well, it paid off, didn't it?' She smiled as she felt the baby kick and saw Doyle's start of surprise when he felt it. 'I think your son is trying to make his presence felt and remind us that he's around.'

Doyle laughed, pressing his hand flat against the mound of the baby, feeling the way it kicked against his palm. 'I don't think there's much danger of us forgetting him, do you? I can still remember how shocked I felt when I found out you were pregnant, honey. It knocked me for six, just the thought of you having my child, yet you weren't even going to tell me about it, were you?'

There was an echo of old pain in Doyle's voice and Gabrielle stared up at him. 'I didn't want you to feel you *had* to do anything. I was in love with you but I knew you didn't love me. I didn't want you to be forced into making any kind of commitment.'

He smoothed her cheek then dropped a light kiss on her mouth. 'Gabby, I was crazy about you! I was smitten from the first moment we met. Henry had told me briefly about you and how worried he was that you were wasting your life, but nothing prepared me for how beautiful you were, how stubborn and infuriating!'

Gabrielle gave a little murmur of protest. 'You could have stopped at "beautiful".'

Doyle laughed. 'But this is the time to tell the truth and bring everything out in the open, sweet. You were all that I said plus so much more that I didn't know whether I was on my head or my heels. No matter how I pushed you, you fought back; you had so much courage and determination. I soon realized that you weren't what I imagined and it scared me because I knew even then that you were becoming far too important to me. I'd been burned once and I didn't intend to be burned again.'

'You're talking about your ex-wife. What was she like Doyle?'

He shrugged, his face suddenly hard. 'Rich, spoilt, wilful, self-centred... Oh, there were faults on both sides, as there are with most marriages which fail. The trouble was that both of us were attracted by the image, not the person beneath. Elaine and I met at an embassy dinner and she was attracted to the uniform as much as to the man wearing it, whereas I thought that she was a beautiful and sophisticated woman.'

'Were you married long?' It hurt to think about it and Gabrielle's voice reflected it.

Doyle swore softly, leading her across the room to sit down on the huge leather chair behind the desk and pull her down on to his knee. He kissed her thoroughly then pressed a finger to her lips to hold the warmth of the kiss a moment longer. 'Don't be hurt, Gabby. It was a long time ago and I never think about Elaine now. But to answer your question, we were married for less than a year until we both finally admitted that it wasn't what we wanted. I would be lying if I said it didn't affect my thinking, but it's so much in the past now that it doesn't matter. You're nothing like Elaine and I don't compare you.'

'I'm glad. I would hate to think that you were thinking of her all the time.' There was a flash of jealousy in Gabrielle's lovely eyes and Doyle laughed as he drew her head down to tease her mouth with fleeting soft kisses.

He paused, his lips a hair's breadth away from hers. 'How could I think of anyone else when you're all I want and need? You plus the child you're going to give me. You will marry me, Gabby, won't you?'

'That depends.' It was her turn to tease now, a small, loving retribution for the torment he was inflicting.

'Depends on what?' His eyes bored into hers, his face tightening. 'Look, I know I don't have the kind of money your family has but by most other standards I'm a wealthy man, Gabrielle. The company is moving from strength to strength!'

She kissed the tip of his nose, smiling at him. 'What a romantic proposal! Sure you aren't going to produce a cash-flow projection to back up your persuasive arguments?' She framed his face with her hands, making him meet her eyes. 'Let's get this clear, Doyle. It's you I love, not your earning potential. Money has never been a consideration for me. As you said before, I could have had my pick of any amount of rich and eligible men, and I picked you because I love you. Understand?'

'I think I'm beginning to. So what is the problem, then?' He drew her down into his arms, holding her gently as he stroked his fingers down her arms to link with her hands and lift them to his mouth to kiss them.

Gabrielle shuddered at the sensations he was creating, trying to force herself to keep her attention on the subject at hand and not let it go drifting off on some tantalising tangent. 'How can I marry you when I don't really know who you are? What does the J.J. stand for?'

'John James,' he replied softly, repeating the light caress. 'Satisfied?'

'Mmm.' Gabrielle snuggled closer, feeling the heat stealing along her veins like fever. 'Almost.'

Doyle caught her meaning at once, his heart pounding heavily under her palm. 'Then I'll have to try a little harder to set your mind at rest, won't I? And once you're completely happy, Gabby, we shall see what we can do about making wedding arrangements. There isn't a lot of time to spare before the baby makes his appearance.'

Doyle's mouth covered hers in a kiss which wiped all thought from her mind, demanding a response that Gabrielle was only too eager to give.

'Er-hem!' The loud voice broke them apart. Gabrielle looked towards the door, colour swimming into her cheeks when she recognised the blond man who had let her in. However, if Doyle felt at all embarrassed by the man's unexpected appearance he gave no sign.

He sighed wearily. 'You always did have a lousy sense of timing, O'Rourke.'

The man grinned, his green eyes filled with amusement as they swept from Doyle to Gabrielle. 'Oh, I wouldn't say that, Major. I reckon my timing is as impeccable as ever.' He drew a bottle of champagne and two glasses from behind his back and walked over to the desk and put them down. 'I would offer to join you in the celebration, but I have the feeling that three would be one too many.'

He sketched them a mocking wave, then left, closing the door carefully behind him. Gabrielle glanced at the bottle, then at the closed door, then back at Doyle. 'Are there many more like him around this place?'

Doyle smiled, reaching for the bottle. 'Don't ask, honey. Let's just say that O'Rourke is one of many whom you will get to know in far too short a time.'

Gabrielle laughed at the wry expression on his face, then gave a tiny gasp when the cork popped free from the bottle with an explosion of sound. Wine fizzed from the neck of the bottle and hurriedly she picked up the glasses so that Doyle could fill them. He put the bottle down again, then looked straight into her eyes. 'Here's to us, Gabby—all three of us and the future we shall have together. That deserves a celebration, don't you think?'

Gabrielle touched her glass to his and took a sip of the pale bubbles, then set the glass down on the desk. Reaching over, she lifted Doyle's glass from his hand

and put it next to hers. 'I agree. But I can think of an even better way to celebrate, can't you?'

Doyle's mouth quirked as he drew her close. 'No wonder I love you, Gabby; you're a woman after my own heart.'

Gabrielle smiled as his mouth touched hers. She drew back a fraction. 'All I ever wanted, Doyle, was your heart—from the moment I was beset by that crazy jungle fever!'

And then there was no need for words...

Temptation

Lost Loves

'Right Man...Wrong time'

All women are haunted by a lost love—a disastrous first romance, a brief affair, a marriage that failed.

A second chance with him...could change everything.

Lost Loves, a powerful, sizzling mini-series from Temptation continues in May 1995 with...

**What Might Have Been
by Glenda Sanders**

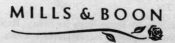

MILLS & BOON

TASTY FOOD COMPETITION!

How would you like a years supply of Temptation books ABSOLUTELY FREE? Well, you can win them! All you have to do is complete the word puzzle below and send it in to us by 31st October 1995. The first 5 correct entries picked out of the bag after that date will win a years supply of Temptation books (*four books every month - worth over £90*). What could be easier?

```
H O L L A N D A I S E R
E Y E G G O W H A O H A
R S E E C L A I R U C T
B T K K A E T S I F I A
E E T I S M A L C F U T
U R C M T L H E E L Q O
G S I U T F O N O E D U
N H L S O T O N E F M I
I S R S O M A C W A A L
R I A E E T I R J A E L
E F G L L P T O T V R E
M O U S S E E O D O C P
```

CLAM	HOLLANDAISE	OYSTERS	SPICE
COD	JAM	PRAWN	STEAK
CREAM	LEEK	QUICHE	TART
ECLAIR	LEMON	RATATOUILLE	
EGG	MELON	RICE	**PLEASE TURN**
FISH	MERINGUE	RISOTTO	**OVER FOR**
GARLIC	MOUSSE	SALT	**DETAILS**
HERB	MUSSELS	SOUFFLE	**ON HOW**
			TO ENTER

HOW TO ENTER

All the words listed overleaf, below the word puzzle, are hidden in the grid. You can find them by reading the letters forward, backwards, up or down, or diagonally. When you find a word, circle it or put a line through it, the remaining letters (which you can read from left to right, from the top of the puzzle through to the bottom) will ask a romantic question.

After you have filled in all the words, don't forget to fill in your name and address in the space provided and pop this page in an envelope (you don't need a stamp) and post it today. Hurry – competition ends 31st October 1995.

Temptation Tasty Food Competition,
FREEPOST,
P.O. Box 344,
Croydon,
Surrey. CR9 9EL

Hidden Question _____

_____

Are you a Reader Service Subscriber? Yes ❑ No ❑

Ms/Mrs/Miss/Mr _____

Address _____

_____

_____ Postcode _____

One application per household.

COMP395